Vampires

Romance to Rippers

An Anthology of

Risqué Stories

Vampires Romance to Rippers

Indie Publishing House

GAINESVILLE, FL

ISBN: 978-1-940871-03-5

LICENSE NOTES

PUBLISHER'S NOTE

This is a work of fiction. Names, characters, places, animate or inanimate objects, or incidents mentioned are either the products of the author's imagination or are used fictitiously, and any resemblance to actual persons, living or dead, business establishments, events, or locales is strictly unintentional and entirely coincidental.

WARNING

EXPLICIT ADULT CONTENT

These stories are considered paranormal romance with fantasy and erotica elements. They are for mature audiences only. They may contain adult language, violence, and strong sexual content including, light bondage situations voyeurism, ménage, and masturbation. All characters depicted in these stories are 18 years or older and all sexual activities are of a consensual nature.

Vampires
Romance to Rippers
An Anthology of Risqué Stories
Table of Contents

Dedication

To Charity Parkerson

Thank you for being my first Indie author buddy. You are a true talent. Before I ever published one word you were the first to agree to participate in this anthology. Thank you for having the faith and confidence that I could pull all of this together. You mean the world to me.

and

To Joseph

What can I say to you to convey all that you mean to me? All of the love, support, and encouragement you have given to me over the years have allowed me the freedom to realize my dreams. You will always and forever be my number one Cutie Pie. I love you, now and always. Thank you for making my world a happier, brighter, and sexier place.

EXPLORING VAMPIRE SEX

By

Bertena Varney

When asked to write this introduction for a book on vampire romance and erotic stories, I decided to take it as a challenge and also an academic endeavor. Now, if any of you were wondering why this would be a challenge or an academic endeavor, well, it's because honestly, I am a little prudish. I can't read the sex scenes in these stories without my face turning red due to embarrassment. The explicitly described images of these stories are seared in my mind and make me stutter. They are so hot that I feel as if I am all dirty as I read these stories of love, lust, and hot sex. Yes, I am almost forty-two years old, but the idea of "sex" graphically described in a book or even a movie just freaks me out, so writing an introduction to this book is stepping into a world of the uncomfortable, yet somehow sinfully inviting.

As many of you know, I have studied vampires academically for a few decades. My studies include the mythological monstrous vampires that were used to explain death, disease, and plagues. I have studied the historical murderous vampires who, in turn, were just humans who were psychopaths that loved blood and murder. I am comfortable with gore and blood. But, while studying vampires, I found that literature is where the vampires began to morph into creatures that were less monstrous and more human. They began to take on human characteristics and seek redemption that leads to sweaty sex and, sometimes, romantic relationships.

So, for academic purposes (wink wink), I have read the stories in this book to find the reason why this is a must-have book on vampire romance and (blush) sex. Here is what I have found.

Vampires have always been a metaphor for sex and taboo actions between a human and a monster. This monster is part of our deepest self that seduces us to let our dark side out and to allow the erotic to come through. Whether it was the great Victorian literature piece, *Dracula*, or the violently dark, *Varney the Vampire: Feast of Blood*, the vampire is the one thing that we know we should not want, but can't live without - just one bite.

In *Varney the Vampire: Feast of Blood* by Sir Thomas Prest (1847), the true nature of the raping monster who took joy in actually feeding and being a vampire is shown. Varney was the first to leave two puncture wounds in the neck and would, without remorse, kill and rape for blood. He is a monster with a tortured soul, but the sex scenes are definitely written by a male, with the focus on the male's need and the fact that he is a monster with only thoughts of what he needs at that moment and no thought towards his victim.

Here is a sample from a sex scene in *Varney the Vampire: Feast of Blood:*

In the beginning was a bald monster with a long face, pointed ears and chin, elongated fingers and sharp talon claws, which lost its humanity and control over its monstrous side. It was lured to a young maiden's window. All of a sudden, with a sudden rush that could not be foreseen and with a strange howling cry that was enough to awaken the terror in any beast, the figure seized the long tresses of hair.

He held her to the bed...she screams...shrieks...and he seizes her neck in his fang like teeth... a gush of blood and a hideous sucking noise follows.

This picture shows rape and torture as the author illustrated the vampire as a sexual monster who wanted to devour women - women who were portrayed as very passive and weak. In these stories, the vampire bite was a metaphor for rape and the monster wanted his victim aware of every agonizing violation. This is the vampire that was created when men ruled the horror world: a creature cursed to walk the

Earth for eternity, searching not for love, but for food.

In *Dracula*, we read about the group sex between the three female vampires and Jonathan Harker, as well as the scene with Lucy, who is very promiscuous and juggles three male suitors. The scene where she is killed is very erotic and has been likened to gang rape. The image is simply three men taking a stake and penetrating her body violently and continuously. Again, the woman is passive and a victim to the men's need.

But, the most erotic scene in *Dracula* is when Mina is forced to drink Dracula's blood from his chest. It is a form of reverse breast-feeding that shows Dracula not only as the provider of life, but the receiver of pleasure. At this time, the Count is an example of uncontrollable lust that is powerful, aggressive, and primal in nature. He is simply an example of parasitic love and a taboo of that time. She is totally under his control.

Today, these stories of rape and torture and submissive women are gone. Women have taken over the vampire literature genre and have introduced readers to a new image of the vampire, one who still hates being a cursed monster and seeks his soul mate, the one woman that after centuries that can not only save his doomed soul, but also satiate his taste for sex. Heck, think about a vampire who has had countless lovers over the centuries, but now only wants to share this experience with you, not just for tonight, but for eternity.

The women in these stories are not submissive victims, but instead are very empowering and strong characters. They walk alongside the vampire in their journey rather than taking on the role of damsel in distress or the hapless victim of his sexual prowess. The current trend for this new genre of vampire romance literature is one that offers the readers an escape from the pressures of the real world while delivering to them either a soul mate or an erotic lover in the form of a vampire.

Here is an excerpt from my fellow author Terri Reid from her short story "More Than Friends" in *Vampires Romance to Rippers: An Anthology of Tasty Stories.*

He moved toward her into the glow of a streetlight and she nearly gasped aloud. As it was, her body reacted with a primitive awakening that surprised and even frightened her.

He bit back a smile. He could hear the blood throbbing quickly through her veins, could feel the rise in her body temperature and could smell the sweet pheromones her body was producing to lure him even closer. She was partially aroused by him, but fighting it. And he was charmed by her efforts.

"I was a few cars down," he said, pointing to a car parked near hers. "I dropped my keys and I was bending over, so I could understand how you might have missed me when you walked to your car. I just came over to make sure you were safe."

Safe. She had never felt so unsafe in her life.

"I'm fine," she said, relieved that the words came out clipped and firm.

"Excellent," he replied, with a full smile. "And now, perhaps we could find a quiet place where I could answer your other question."

Eyes narrowed, she shook her head. "Other question?"

He stepped even closer and she held her ground. He was not going to intimidate her.

Reaching forward, he ran a finger down the side of her face and she shivered involuntarily and swallowed slowly. "Where I came from," he whispered, his breath hot on her cheek, "Originally."

She took a deep shuddering breath and stepped back, away from him. "Listen," she replied, her voice uneven. "I don't know who you are or what you think you're doing. But I am not a hooker, I'm a police officer. I'm a detective. So unless you want to spend a little time in a cooling cell, I would suggest you step away and take your advances elsewhere."

His lips lifted in a half smile, but he didn't move back. "I know you're not a hooker, Detective Victory," he said, meeting her eyes. "And the only proposition I have for you right now, is an offer to help you track down the person who is killing those women who have requested to be your friend."

"What the..." her hand went to her gun, but he stepped even closer and laid his hand over hers, blocking her attempt. Her back was pressed against the side of her car and her hand was caught between her body and his. And the heat coursing through her veins was making her feel lightheaded.

"I'm not here to harm you," he whispered, keeping an eye out for other police officers who might be coming off shift...bending his head, he drew his mouth along the underside of her jaw line and a bolt of heat impaled her core, turning her legs to rubber. She collapsed against the side of her car and he pressed his body fully against hers.

"Did you drug me?" she murmured, trying to fight the sexual haze that was overwhelming her. "I feel..."

He slid his hands up the sides of her body, slowly, caressing every curve, the power of passion clouding his own judgment. "You feel delightful," he breathed, his mouth hovering just inches over hers. "You feel exactly the way I've dreamt you'd feel."

Now that women are the dominant writers of vampire literature, the vampires have evolved into a sexual, romantic bad boy of the night: they are the soul mate, the erotic lover, and the escape that many women look for in today's world. The characters and their readers fall in love with these charismatic and seductive monsters that display superhuman abilities. These vampires, by nature, can seduce the lead female character, defeat death, and physically destroy their enemies to protect their lover. This is very seductive to the reader.

The reader, as well as the new female lead character, has evolved into a financially independent person that can provide for herself. She is no longer the buxom blonde that is hapless and sex crazed, but more of a girl-next-door type that the vampire finds so mysteriously alluring. She gets into trouble, but does not need rescuing. Instead, she assists in the adventure. She is her own hero and experiences this adventure equally with the vampire at her side.

These women dream of forbidden acts of sex and romance that can only be provided to them by the alluring vampire. They want an immortal and indestructible hero that can sweep them off their feet, romance them, and sex their brains out while being theirs forever. The vampire offers the bad boy appeal that most women have longed for at one time. They respect the female character as a person, but at the same time, they want to protect and care for her. For many readers, this is the quandary that they face today - trying to balance being both independent yet sexually attractive. They want to prove that they can do anything that they want to, but also let everyone know that just because they can do it all, it does not mean that they have to do it all. They want that immortal, indestructible lover to be there and to sweep them off their feet after a long day at work. They want to escape for their world.

But, most importantly, the vampires need these women. They empower them to push themselves to the limits; since vampires can experience complete freedom, they in turn pass this freedom on to their lovers. But, these bad boys are often flawed in some way and they need these women to fix them. They are weak in regards to these women and, in the end, these strong vampires will give their power over to the females – the one person that can save their souls and satiate their lust. In the end, the women are the strong heroes of the stories.

The vampire romance genre can range from mildly erotic to explicitly erotic. Women are not usually the consumers of film or print pornography because most usually are not visually stimulated. Women tend to lean towards written scenes to satisfy their real life desire; the words on the page provide images in their minds that women can integrate into their real life and with their real relationships. These vampire romance stories range from slightly

23

titillating to full-blown erotica, with no holds barred, blushing, and even "Oh my God" responses (especially for this reader). But, no matter the extent of the vampire book, the vampire is there to please the woman in whatever ways she wants. He is at her mercy.

Vampires are the new heroes of romance novels. They offer a soul mate concept with a lifetime of sexual experiences that is focused purely on the female. They offer escapism for the reader who is bored with her life as it is. These new authors of vampire erotica will continue to bring their vampires into our bedrooms to please us in many ways. These sexual beings will always be in the shadows of our dreams as well as forming our choices in our current mate or our search for one. Many readers wish for them to be floating outside their window and to have a chance to let them in, even if for just one night. This need for escapism will guarantee that vampires are here to stay.

So, as you explore the hot titillating pages of these stories searching for your soul mate or just your one night erotic lover, I will be reading as well, but with my eyes covered and peeking through my fingers. So, for now I am going to continue my ... errr uhmmm ... academic research and get back to reading these stories.

Goodnight for now and naughty dreams to all!

About the Author

Bertena Varney is an avid vampire fan that has made these creatures of the night not only a hobby but also an academic study. She has studied the historical, mythological, and pop cultural aspect of the vampire throughout her undergraduate and graduate career. During one of her master's programs, she participated in independent studies on vampires. She then turned this research into her book *Lure of the Vampire: A Pop Culture Reference Book.* Once it gained popularity as a self-published book, it was picked up by Hydra Publications, and republished with new material and re-titled *Lure of the Vampire- Revamped.*

She has also collaborated with young adult author, Elizabeth Loraine, in writing her fiction book *Lillian: A Vampire Story.* Recently, she has worked with Stavros and his company Crazy Duck, where she contributed to and edited *Vampire News 2011: Tasty Bits You Can*

Sink Your Fangs Into and *Vampire News 2012: The Not So End Times Edition.*

Other contributions include *The Sirens Compendium* and *The Witching Hour: A Harry Potter Convention Compendium,* which includes selected papers of presentations that she has attended.

She has toured across the country and presented at various conferences, conventions, festivals, libraries, colleges, and more. She is also a contributor to Examiner.com, where she holds the title of Vampire Examiner, True Blood Examiner, Book and Movie Examiner, and many more.

She currently teaches sociology and mass media at Southcentral Kentucky Community and Technical College. She is a graduate of Morehead State University from which she holds a B.A. and M.Ed. in Social Science and Education, and an M.A. in Sociology and Criminology. She has one adult son, Tre', and currently lives in Bowling Green, KY with her boyfriend Sam and their kitty Luna.

She is a member of two non-profits: one is The D20 Girls Project and the other is The Modified Dolls. Both empower females to embrace their difference either through their geekiness or their body modification and show society that beauty is diverse.

Bertena Varney, M.A., M.Ed.

SEXING THE DARK

BY

J.B. Stilwell

I was a normal child, for the most part. One thing that made me different was my love for writing. I was the kid in middle school who would squeal in delight with writing assignments and essay questions. You can just imagine how popular that made me. Still, even with the disapproving looks from classmates, I escaped into my own world: imagining fantastical stories, writing, and, of course, reading everything I could.

It was during this time that I read the book that would forever change my life – Mary Shelley's *Frankenstein*. You might be thinking, wait J.B., you write about vampires. How could *Frankenstein* lead you down that path?

For me, Mary Shelley's iconic novel did for me what would later be further developed by the works of Gene Roddenberry. Shelley's work was my first conscious exposure to the use of literary fiction as social commentary, using the monster as a way to express the dangers of good science used for evil gains, but also as the juxtaposition for working through Dr. Frankenstein's own existential crisis.

Although I was young, I saw unlimited possibilities for using monsters to explore the religious, philosophical, social, and personal issues that confounded me – much like Roddenberry's *Star Trek* did for TV viewers. The use of monsters (or aliens with Roddenberry) for this purpose provides a somewhat safer platform for discourse. Instead of bluntly directing criticism on certain issues that humans face, using fictional, non-human characters provides a way to criticize without implication – to safely process these issues from a distance. We can explore the darkest issues of human nature, but still feel good about ourselves because we're talking about monsters. Still, the impact of the paranormal and science fiction genres is just as great, particularly when the story telling is so good that we can see glimpses of ourselves in those non-human characters. It's even better when we can feel sympathy for the darkness – that's when you know you have discovered a great artist, like Shelley and Roddenberry.

Around this same time, I revisited a classic movie that my family used to watch on a home projector – the original *Dracula,* starring Bela Lugosi. Unlike *Frankenstein's* monster, who was made up of body parts, Dracula was once human. He was a human transformed into a being who exhibited the worst parts of human behavior. He was a predator, a murderer, a master manipulator, and overall, a dastardly fiend. Even more frightening, through his unique vampire powers, Dracula was able to hypnotize his "victims" (term used loosely here) so that they seemingly offered their necks willingly.

I was enthralled. The idea of *choosing* to do bad things intertwined with raging teenage hormones made for the vampire to be a regular source of budding sexual excitement. What was it about this fiend that had my blood rushing and skin flushed in anticipation?

From this point on, I recognized this strange and exciting pull whenever seeing a movie or reading a story about vampires. The thought of danger, of literally dancing with the possibility of death within the safety of a story, was the best adrenaline rush. These reactions not only stimulated me, but I also became curious as to why I was so seduced by vampires – not to mention the scores of other fans who felt the exact same pull.

Why are vampires so damn sexy? I never had this reaction with *Frankenstein's* monster, so what's different? These questions plagued me so much as a young girl, that I read everything I could get my hands on – vampire fiction, mythology, and literary critiques. What I learned from all of these texts provided an explanation for the sexual explosion I was feeling. Vampires can be used as a metaphor for many of the darker human behaviors, but it's the representation of the basest of human desires that attracts us all.

Let's look specifically at the male vampire. Just think of it. You must *invite* him into your home, making you a willing participant. He caresses and seduces you with his eyes, mind, and body, expressing a deep *need* to consume you. His goal is to ravage your body in a way that only he can, using expert techniques of foreplay to build your anticipation until you surrender yourself completely, begging for release. Once he has you at that pinnacle, he thrusts his fangs into you, penetrating the fiber of your very existence. Even more so, his very sustenance, what allows him to live is *your* blood, your life essence. Without you, he could not exist. He *needs* you. In terms of a sexual relationship, two bodies join. But, with the vampire, he can't thrive by mere joining. He must completely take you *into* him, drawing in the very energy of your vitality so that he can *be*.

From your part, regardless of the naughtiest things you do "willingly," you can continue on guilt free because your complicity was really coercion. You enjoyed it, you had pleasure beyond your wildest dreams and you might even desire to do it all again – even when you know others would be shocked and possibly disgusted. No worries, because it wasn't really your fault. You need not be ashamed because you only did what you did because of vampire powers directing your will.

You can embrace your sexuality and NOT feel badly about it. This is the freedom that vampire fiction gives us as women. Many of us live in cultures that at varying degrees repress female sexuality. Vampire stories even express this through the use of religious symbolism to protect against being a "victim." Embrace the church and you can ward off vampires, just like many religious institutions condemn pleasures of the flesh.

No more. With the vampire, you can live out your most secret fantasies without retribution. And with the female vampire, women can live vicariously through a strong woman figure who not only embraces her sexuality, but is the ultimate initiator, dominating her partners in a way that only the vampire can – with a firm grace that no other monster can match.

Some would argue that approaching the vampire character in such a way supports a type of rape culture. No reasonable person with any ethical standards would argue that rape – real or imagined – is okay. This essay cannot fully address this critique. I will only say this - the use of the vampire in fiction is not about victimization, although it may appear so from the most simplistic analysis. Vampires free us to explore ourselves more than what our cultures deem allowable. It is because of this that the vampire has survived through the ages, with millions of vampire fiction fans worldwide. We can live the fantasy that seems too daring – or even inappropriate – to examine in our everyday lives.

This freedom to explore is one of many reasons why I choose to write about vampires. As a writer, not only can I delve into these feelings and desires more for myself, I can also use my characters to provide readers an opportunity to think of these issues themselves. And maybe along the way, the fantasy will inspire us to be the sexual beings we are meant to be. Enjoy it; you deserve the pleasure.

Fang on!

HOT DARK COMFORT

A Sexier Modified Excerpt from

Mining the Dark

By

J.B. Stilwell

"Can you give a little more help? I thought vampires were supposed to have uber-strength or something."

As soon as I say it, Rick quickly lifts the entire recliner, almost pulling it out of my hands.

"Thanks," I grumble.

"My pleasure," he responds.

Not exactly my idea of a great way to spend a Saturday night – moving my remaining stuff out of my mom's large storage shed. Before working on the Federal Office of Human and Vampire Administration project, I didn't intend on moving to Rowan, West Virginia. Many of my possessions have been sitting in Huntington, gathering dust. It will be nice to be surrounded by my own things again. My new apartment will actually feel like home. Thankfully, my project partner and now co-worker, Dr. Rick Allstedt, graciously offered to help with the move. It's even nicer that he's a vampire and can carry heavier loads. Just sucks that we have to do all of this work after the sun goes down. I guess it could be worse. The sun could be blazing in the winter sky and my clothes could be wet with cold sweat. Oh, and Rick would be a pile of gelatinous muck. So, yeah, this is better.

We lift the recliner into the back of the moving van and return to the shed for the boxes of smaller items. My mom steps outside from the back of her house. Ambling toward us, she says, "Do y'all want some lemonade?"

I look at Rick and smile.

"Thanks, Mrs. Burcham. Lemonade would be nice," Rick says.

My mouth drops open as my mom walks back to the house. "I thought you didn't need to drink human stuff?" I ask.

"I don't," he responds. "Doesn't mean that I can't. I partake every once in a while. Especially when a nice Appalachian woman offers me something for all of my hard work. Well, at least offers me more than a hard time." He raises an eyebrow at me.

I take my box to the truck while stating, "You didn't have to come. No one twisted your arm. I couldn't if I tried anyhow."

He slides his box into the truck, then leans against the bumper, smiling. "You know you couldn't do this without me."

I roll my eyes. "I so could have. And probably would have had less aggravation, too."

"And less distraction, too," he quips. "I'm sure your other help wouldn't have been as attractive as me." He winks, then walks back to the shed.

I stand there, hands outstretched in exasperation. I decide not to egg him on. One thing I've learned in the past couple of weeks since we finished the FOHVA project is that if you respond when Rick goads you, it just encourages him to do it even more. It doesn't help that I once let it slip out that I thought he was hot. He likes to throw that up in my face every once in a while. Reliving that humiliation is not my idea of time well spent. But he seems to get a kick out of it. Bastard. And I say that in the most loving way possible.

When I get back to the shed, Rick is already drinking his lemonade and chatting with my mom. Talk about humiliation. The last thing I need is more Emma stories that he'll use to tease me unmercifully in the most awkward of moments.

"Whatcha y'all talking about?" I ask as I reach for my glass of lemonade.

Handing me my glass, Mom says, "Oh, we're just shootin' the breeze."

"Uh-huh," I groan as Rick grins at me. "What?" I ask him.

"Just enjoying the relaxed form of speech you get whenever you're around your mom," he replies.

I whack him on the arm. "Now, Emma Jean, cut that out," Mom scolds me. "Rick came all this way to help ya and that's no way to treat a friend. I taught you better than that."

Rick raises his eyebrows at me. "Sorry, Mom. He can be as hard to deal with as trying to hold onto a greased weasel."

Rick laughs loudly while I resist the urge to throw my empty glass at him. Mom gives me a tough stare, then says, "I still don't understand why y'all couldn't've moved all this stuff during the day, instead of comin' out here so late. It's so dark you'll have a dickens of a time driving back to Rowan."

Rick and I look at one another. My eyes widen as it occurs to me that Mom doesn't know that Rick is a vampire. Rick seemingly understands my thoughts and slightly shrugs his shoulders.

"Uh, Mom? We couldn't come during the day because Rick's a vampire."

She looks at me, then looks at him, then back at me again. Before I can say another word, she ambles up to Rick, standing toe-to-toe with him as she peers up into his face. I steel myself for what is about to happen, hoping that it's not that bad. Rick looks down at my mom with the kindest look on his face.

She clucks her tongue. "Let me see your teeth," she demands quite simply.

He smiles down at her as I gasp, completely horrified. "MOM!" I exclaim.

She turns to me. "What, Emma Jean? I've never met a vampire before. I just want to see." She turns to Rick. "Let me see your teeth."

Rick continues to smile. "My pleasure, Mrs. Burcham." He opens his mouth and his fangs extend out in all their blood-drinking glory.

Mom humphs as she looks closely into his mouth. "Well, I'll be damned. Those things look sharp! I bet you could open a can or bottle of beer with those things!" She looks at me and love taps my arm. "Good thing to have around if you lose your can opener."

Rick laughs good-naturedly. "I'm not sure if I could do that. Might chip a fang." He winks at my mom.

Mom looks back at him. "Well, can't ya just go to the dentist if that happens? They put caps on other teeth. Why can't they cap a fang?"

I roll my eyes, trying not to get too embarrassed at my mom's inquisition. It's like bringing a boyfriend home for the first time. "Mom, please, I'm begging you. Just leave him alone."

Rick shows his exceptional patience. "It's all right, Emma. Jean." He grins. "I'm not sure a doctor could help with these types of teeth.

Since they extend from my gums at certain times, a cap wouldn't work."

Mom looks him up and down. "Docs have used prosthetics on other parts that extend."

"OH MY GOD, Mom, please stop!"

She looks at me again. "What? It's the truth."

Rick laughs. "That it is, Mrs. Burcham. Fortunately for those who need it, that can be done as the part in question is...well, flexible enough that polymer-based synthetic skin would work. Because it can stretch. That's not the case with fangs, which are basically hardened calcium. Which in vampires, they can..." He looks at me. "... get bigger."

"Huh. Well, it's a thought. If doctors can make teeth for me, surely they can come up with something for you in the event ya need it. Maybe y'all can make money in developing the first vampire dentures."

Rick smiles benevolently at her. "Good idea, Mrs. Burcham. I like the way you think."

Mom takes the glasses from us and humphs. "Now y'all finish your work and get on back to Rowan before it gets too late. I'm gonna head on to bed." I hug her good night, then return to the shed for the last couple of boxes, trying to run from the embarrassment of the last few minutes. Rick helps me finish loading the truck, smiling to himself the entire time. At this point, I don't dare ask him what he's smiling about.

We close and lock the hatch to the truck, then situate ourselves in the cab. I'm the lucky one who gets to drive this beast of a vehicle. It's not too much of an aggravation if it's a short distance, but the three-to-four hour drive to Rowan is a little daunting. And so far, Rick hasn't offered to share the driving responsibilities.

Before starting the truck, I look over at him. "Listen, Rick. I really appreciate all of the help you have given me with moving my stuff. I hate to sound ungrateful, but can you drive at least part of the way?"

Rick gives me a droll look. "First, you don't hate to sound ungrateful. You have actually made that a competitive sport."

I stick my tongue out at him. My issues with acting like an angst-ridden teen tend to devolve into childish temper tantrums when I'm tired and emotionally exhausted from trying conversations.

He laughs. "Second, all you have to do is ask. I may know what you're feeling, but that doesn't mean I can read your mind." He leaps from the truck and walks over to the driver's side.

Opening the door, I say, "If you know how I feel, then you know how tired I am. Why not offer to drive instead of making me ask?"

He cocks his head to the side, looking at me like I just made the most ridiculous request. "Emma, one thing I have learned about you is not to assume what you're thinking based on how you're feeling. You are one person who is a perplexing study in emotional contradictions. You rarely think what you feel, much less say what you feel. Besides, I kind of like it when you ask me." He winks.

"Whatever, Rick. It's not like you know me that well." I push against his abdomen with my forearm.

His voice drops to the salacious timbre he has perfected. "Oh, but I know you much better than you realize." Grinning, he hops into the driver's seat. Shaking my head, I let it go and count up my bad thoughts for the week before getting into the passenger's seat.

"Buckle up," he says. "I've never driven one of these things, so I can't guarantee how safely I'll drive."

"Wonderful," I grumble. "You'll have to change how you're always telling me that I'm SAFE in the company of a vampire."

He grins. "And by the way, I'm in no need for prosthetics for any of my parts." He winks at me.

Horrified, I turn away from him and hunker down in my seat. He just laughs as we hit US 60 toward I-64 East toward my new home in Rowan.

Sitting in my recliner, having some hot coffee, and watching the news, I wonder what I can get into on a lazy Sunday. It's my last day off before my first official day with the FOHVA Paranormal Investigations Team. I want to spend this time NOT thinking about things that go bump in the night, but I can't help but think of the project work we completed, particularly the last demonstration with the child vampire. Even after having a long talk with my mom, I still can't let go of the idea that we executed a child. Yes, the child was actually a 103-year-old pedophile vampire, but he still looked like a ten-year-old boy.

I've always known on some level that looks can be deceiving. Yet, that experience with the child vampire was an unequalled example of how sometimes what you think you see is nowhere close to being the truth. I'm still trying to figure out why the universe saw fit to make me live through that event. While I'm also trying not to think about supernatural entities. Yes, my life is not only full of paradoxes, but also a study in ambivalence.

Right now, I think I'll opt for some distraction. I'll think of everything else once it's actually part of my job. In other words, I'm putting it off until tomorrow. For today, getting out and exploring more of Rowan seems like a good idea, even if I have to venture out on my own. Rick won't be getting up until later this evening, and I don't want to waste any precious sun time. Might not get much of it in the near future.

I quickly shower, dress, apply my signature pink lip-gloss and black mascara, then head out to my car. Taking long drives around the county is always relaxing. Since Rowan is far from a metropolitan deluge of stimulation, one can almost go into a meditative state while driving. On second thought, that's not so safe, considering the number of deer and other wild animals bounding across the roads at any given moment. I definitely need to find a new way to relax.

I pull to a stop in front of the local diner, The Soup Spoon. I've neglected to realize that it's Sunday, so many local business are either closed for the day or only open after church services are completed. Well, I guess I can always go to the one place that is always full of activity on the weekends, before, during, and after church – the Rowan Flea Market.

As I head toward the epicenter of friendly and social bartering for goods, I stop at the locally owned gas station, Bobby Joe's Drop 'N Shop. I get out of my car, then suddenly stop to watch a rather attractive man in blue, grease-stained coveralls walk quickly to the side of my car. He nods at me, smiling. "Hi. I'm the only one here right now, so I'll go ahead and pump your gas for you. Want me to fill it up?"

"Oh, yes," I gasp breathily before stammering, "Yes, please. Fill me up, er, fill my car up, yes, please." I quickly turn away from him as the heat of my skin threatens to expose my inner humiliation. I glance over my shoulder to watch him as he busies himself with fully servicing my car – pumping the gas, cleaning the windows, and checking my fluids. This is definitely the type of service you don't find in big cities. I also don't remember ever being serviced by someone quite so beautiful.

Serviced, right. I need to stop thinking like this for the simple fact that I can't trust what might come out of my mouth if he starts talking to me. I try to watch him slyly, appreciating his shaggy, shoulder length black hair bound with a bandana, chiseled masculine bone structure pushing against taut bronze skin that would be the envy of a Greek God. As he squats to check the air in my back tires, I imagine myself running my hands over the fabric that is pulled tight across his muscular back.

The pump clicks to indicate my tank is full, abruptly snapping me out of my reverie. He looks up at me and smiles. "I'm almost done."

I return his smile. "Take your time."

When he finishes everything, he walks over to me and says, "That will be $56.47."

"Ouch," I remark as I hand him my debit card.

Looking at my card, then back up at me, still smiling, he states, "Okay, Emma. I'll be right back."

After a few moments, he returns with my card and a receipt. Taking them from his hand, I say, "Thank you...what's your name?" I'm kicking myself for being so forward, but hey, my only friend in Rowan is someone who sleeps through the day. I'll take a chance and hopefully not make a fool out of myself.

"My name's David. I would shake your hand, but I'm covered in grease." He holds up his hands, turning them from side-to-side and, for the first time, I notice the multiple tattoos snaking up both of his arms.

I pull my eyes away from his forearms. "Nice to meet you, David. Thanks for the thorough job you did on my car."

"My pleasure. And with these gas prices, you deserve all the servicing you can get."

"Yes, good service does help the feeling of getting screwed." I bite my lip and briefly close my eyes as I mentally kick myself. I am *so* mentally challenged right now.

David laughs good-naturedly. "No truer words have been spoken. Well, I've got to get back to fixing another car." He walks toward the garage before turning back to say, "It really was a pleasure to meet you, Emma."

I smile broadly as I get back into my car, willing my legs to stop shaking. I'm back at my apartment before my breathing returns to normal and I realize, dang, I completely forgot about going to the flea market. I guess Rowan is full of more distractions than I realized.

I decide to busy myself with housework and reading while I wait for the sun to go down. At least Rick is somewhat used to my nonsensical chitchat. At least with him, I'm less likely to feel overly self-conscious about making a fool out of myself. I mean, he's seen me passed out, splattered in blood *twice,* and still doesn't treat me like a pariah. I'll take my good luck where I can get it, and Rick has been quite a charm in more ways than one.

When the sun sets, I open the front door, expecting to see Rick climbing the external stairs. I glance around the apartment complex and don't see anyone moving around the building. Right as I'm shutting the door, Rick pushes it open. I grip the doorknob as I grit my teeth. "Why don't you announce yourself? One of these times, you're going to do that and I'm going to have a stake in my hand. I won't be responsible for what happens after that." I take the charm comment back.

Grinning, he strolls into my apartment. "Been waiting for me long?" he asks.

Rolling my eyes, I plop down on the couch. "I was hardly waiting for you."

"So you often look outside your front door after the sun sets?"

"Only since I learned that the bogeyman is real." I stick my tongue out at him as my face scrunches into a scowl.

He laughs as he makes himself comfortable in my recliner. Resting his hands behind his head, he states, "Our last free night before we start our new jobs as paranormal investigators."

I sit on the couch and try to relax. "Yep, the big day. I wonder what we'll have to investigate first."

He looks at me, suddenly very serious. "Are you ready for this?"

"Sure. Why wouldn't I be?"

He gives me an oh-give-me-a-break glare. "Okay," I respond. "I'm nervous because it's going to be the first day. And yes, I'm hesitant about just how I will react to things."

Nodding, he says, "That's to be expected."

"How do you mean?"

He leans forward in the recliner, rubbing his hands together. "Well, the project was very emotional. For all of us. You were dealing with a lot of situations that you probably never thought you would have to deal with. And it was traumatic. Especially…"

"Especially the last demonstration."

"Right. How are you holding up?"

"Rick, I told you before that I don't want to talk about it."

"Want and need are two different things," he offers, his voice low and caring.

I look down at my lap. "I have talked about things. With Mom."

"Good. I'm glad that you're not bottling things up. Did you tell her everything?"

Twisting my hands together as I make a show of examining my fingers, I say, "Not exactly."

"Meaning?"

I look at him, exasperated. "Well, it's not like I could give her the details of a top-secret project. Still, it was helpful."

Rick moves to the couch, sitting close, but not too close. He rests his arm on the couch behind me. "Helpful is always…helpful. Was it enough to make you feel more comfortable about things?"

I look up at him. "Sort of. What I *don't* want to do is relive the experience."

"But you do."

I scowl. "I do NOT. I don't ever want to relive that."

He shakes his head slowly. "I know you don't *want* to, but even if you don't talk about it, you're still reliving it on the inside." He takes my hand. "I told you before. You don't have to do everything yourself. I was there. I know what happened. I will be able to relate to things. If we talk about them."

"Rick, I really don't want to do this..." I start to get up, but he grabs my arms and holds me down. I try to jerk away from him, but it's completely pointless against his vampire strength. "Rick, just let go of me!" I yell.

He pulls me flush against his body. Breathing heavily, I continue to struggle against him. "Let go!" He leans closer to me, speaking slowly in that hypnotic way he does. "Never," he says as his eyes dart over my face. "I will never let go. Not while you're hurting. And when I *know* I can help."

I stop struggling, my eyes still narrowed in anger. "It's. Not. Your. Place."

He pulls me into a softer embrace, voice still low. "Look at it this way," he says while searching my face. "We're on the same team. I know that at least part of the time, your head is somewhere else. And until you deal with it, you are going to be a liability on any work we do.

Consider it me helping myself, if that helps you get through the night."

I push him away, and he doesn't resist. I scoot over to the arm of the couch, running my hand through my hair. I can't seem to find the words to say what I need him to hear.

He rests his hand, palm up, on the couch beside me. He whispers, "Emma...please."

I run my hand over my face, masking the wetness of my eyes. "Um, look. I don't feel comfortable talking to you about it." Quiet fills the room for several moments. I drop my hand and look at him. He's staring at me, mouth slightly open. He actually looks hurt.

I try to explain. "You're too close to the situation. It's like, you know me, sort of. But you don't know me that well. And I just feel that I can't talk to you...without some type of judgment. Or you thinking differently about me."

He purses his lips into a severely thin line. "If you think so little of me," he begins, "as a friend. As a colleague. Then, Emma dear, I think your issues are much deeper than either one of us realized."

He abruptly stomps toward the door. I jump up. "Rick, wait!" He stops, his back still turned toward me. Now I can't stop the tears. I begin sobbing. "I don't know what I'm saying. I'm not explaining it right. I just can't. I can't. It's all I think about. It's like, if I talk about it, it's really real. And with you. You were there. You can confirm my nightmares. That I did it. That I'm…I'm a…child killer!"

I drop to the floor, sobbing hysterically. I feel strong arms wrapped around me. I bury my face into his chest and just let the tears run down my face. No more holding it in, now that the dam has broken.

Rick continues to hold me. He whispers, "He wasn't a child. He was a vampire."

I look up into his face, tears streaming down my cheeks. I shake my head and groan, "If he's not a child…then you're not a man."

Sadness sweeps over his eyes as he forces a heart sore smile. "I'm not a man, Emma. I'm a vampire."

I shake my head more. "You're a man to me. And if you're a man…then I killed a child." I look at his chest, staring at nothing in particular.

Rick's chest heaves as he takes a deep, fake vampire breath. "I wish it were that simple. I was a man. Now I'm something different. I guess I'm still a man. And something more. Just like Henry was a child. And something more." He leans back against the couch, pulling me against his torso so that I'm resting between his outstretched legs. He continues, "You can put any label you want on us. We're both vampires. But there's still one major difference. He was a murderer. I'm not. Behavior doesn't necessarily determine identity, unless one chooses to become that which is done. And Henry did. He didn't murder. He *was* murder. And rape. And torture. And it wasn't like something he did once and then repented. He did it over and over again. Multiple times. For decades. And he enjoyed it. He was the child killer. Not you."

I listen to him earnestly as the tears begin to slow. I look up into his face, daring to let a little hope into my heart.

He briefly smiles. "Like I've said before, the fact that you don't enjoy it, that you question the *rightness* of it all. That's what makes you one of the good guys. And just as important, it's what distinguishes you from one of the bad guys." He slowly leans forward and kisses my forehead.

I look at him, waiting for any more pearls of wisdom. He just continues to watch me, as if he's wondering if I will stay or run. I rest my head against his chest, breathing deeply as I try to recount each word that he has said. I plan on using them as my personal mantra when I begin to second-guess myself.

I stretch out between his legs, still repeating his words in my mind. Rick continues to hold me, but not tightly like before - just enough for me to be comfortable and not slide away from him. Many moments pass and I slowly ebb into sweet, dreamless sleep.

I wake up with a start. It's pitch black, but I can tell that I'm in my bed. At least, I think it's my bed. I turn the bedside lamp on and breathe a sigh of relief as I recognize the furniture and thick window dressings of my own room. Thank God, I didn't wake up in someone else's bed. It's a first for me saying that. Go figure.

I suddenly remember what happened and look around the bedroom floor to see if Rick had taken up residence again. I quickly grab all over my body to make sure that I'm fully clothed. I need to figure out why I'm always ending up unconscious and waking to horrible thoughts of Rick undressing me, either to clean vampire goo or get me ready for bed. Either way, not ready to give a peep show. Well, maybe not ready.

I kneel down on the floor to look under the bed. Yep, Rick is sleeping soundly. At least he didn't scare the hell out of me this time.

I walk quietly toward the kitchen, intent on making a late afternoon breakfast. Before I know what's happening, I'm pressed against the wall in the back corner of the bedroom. Rick has his arms wrapped tightly around me, his fingers kneading my lower back. His lips are on mine, his tongue forcing my lips apart. I'm stunned. It's like all of it is just happening to me, with very little reaction.

Maybe it is the solace I have found in Rick or the excitement of flirting with David. Either way, finding more comfort in Rick seems like the best idea I've had in a long time.

Rick easily lifts me, his hands cupping my buttocks, and carries me to the bedroom. He lays me gently on the bed, pressing himself between my legs as he continues to kiss down my neck to the bare flesh at the top of my chest. "Um, Rick?"

He groans against my skin. "Uuuuhhhh-hhhhhmmmm?"

I tightly squeeze my eyes shut. "I don't have any protection."

His head jerks up as he looks at me. "I'm not capable of getting you pregnant." He begins kissing my lips again.

I moan against him. "What about other…stuff?"

He raises one eyebrow. "What other stuff?"

Feeling more than slightly embarrassed, I mumble, "Like…viruses?"

He smiles broadly. "I love that you would take care of yourself like that." He kisses the tip of my nose. "With vampire healing and immunity, I'm also not capable of passing any known viruses."

"Oh, thank God!" I exclaim a little too excitedly.

He chuckles before lightly caressing my face with his fingertips. He brushes his thumb across my bottom lip as he kisses below my ear. He licks and lightly sucks his way back down to the bare area of my chest, his hand moving from my face to the hem of my shirt. He skims his hands over my abdomen as he lifts the cloth up and over my head. Tossing my shirt to the floor, he begins kissing the exposed areas of my breasts, my nipples erect and pressing against the lace of my bra. He runs his tongue along the edge of the lace while one hand twists and flicks my nipple.

I arch my back as he continues kissing down my stomach as he rolls my nipples between his fingers. He runs his tongue along the band of my slacks before quickly unfastening the buttons and sliding them over my hips and down my legs. He grins as he looks at me lying there, naked except for my bra and panties.

Taking one of my feet in his hands, he kisses my ankle before slowly running his tongue up the back of my calf. He pauses at the back of my knee, running his lips over my skin while his hand massages my other leg, fingers leisurely tracing around my thigh. His lips inch up to my hip, then he smoothly kisses across the lace-covered mound of my sex. He stops and breathes in deeply, relishing the scent. He runs his tongue inside my waistband, torturing me with his teasing before he hooks his fangs into my panties and swiftly rips them from my body.

I squeal in astonishment and delight. He grins up at me before becoming a blur of motion. Before I know it, he's completely naked and kneeling between my legs. The hard length of his manhood juts out in eager anticipation of what's to come next. He carefully positions himself between my legs as he crushes his mouth against mine, his fangs dangerously close to drawing blood. He grinds his hips into mine before snaking his arms around me and deftly unhooking my bra. He quickly removes it and tosses it to the floor with the rest of our clothes.

He lies down on top of me, the full weight of his body melding into mine. Both of his hands rest beside my head, playing with my hair as he stares down at me. He moves his hips so that his hardness slides easily between the folds of my sex. He kisses lightly all over my face while his hips swivel and rock, his manhood rubbing firmly and deliciously against that sweetest of spots causing my nub to throb and pulse against him. He continues this rhythm as his mouth suckles at my breasts. I begin panting, the pressure building between my hips. Right as I feel like I'm going to explode, he quickly slides down and thrusts inside of me causing me to scream out as I ride wave after wave of pleasure.

Instead of thrusting to a finish, Rick slows down and grits his teeth as my muscles squeeze his massive girth. He sucks my nipple far into his mouth until the tip is rubbing against the opening to his throat, nearly swallowing me whole while I continue to groan loudly.

He resumes his thrusting in an achingly slow pace, taking his time as he lavishes my upper body with his mouth and tongue. His rhythm quickens until we're both panting. He grips the sheets tightly before he thrusts hard three, four more times and spills inside of me. As his length continues to throb, he relaxes and rests his head on my shoulder.

He slides out and drops to my side, pulling me into a spooning position. Without either of us saying a word, we bask in the warmth of our bodies, both of us teetering near the edge of more sleep. He kisses the back of my neck, grazing his fangs against my skin. He runs his tongue over the burning area. Did he just take a taste? I run my hand over the red stickiness of my chest. Taste or not, I'm not really caring right now. I snuggle more tightly against him as he rubs his face against my hair.

Damn. We should really be getting ready to go to the research facility. It will be hard to work without a knowing grin on my face. Think anyone will notice? Lying in the bed with all types of wicked thoughts running through my mind, I'm tempted to leave the blood on me, knowing full well that other vampires will be able to smell it. I close my eyes at the thought and wrap his arms tightly around me.

About the Author

J.B. Stilwell is a paranormal romance/thriller novelist who published her debut novel *The Source* in 2012 and is working on the sequel *Mining the Dark* to be released at the end of 2013. These books are the first "The Mountain State Vampire Series," a collection of paranormal novels set in the mountains of West Virginia.

J.B. was born and raised in the foothills of Appalachia and currently resides in the Seattle metropolitan area with her husband and daughter. She has eclectic interests that show in her writing. J.B. has a degree in Sociology; her studies focused on crime/deviant behavior for undergrad and race/gender relations in post-grad. She loves to travel, particularly to India, and her varied experiences around the world are woven into her stories.

Aside from writing, she loves to read, listen to music, watch good TV/movies, crochet, and above all else, spend time with family and friends.

A STROKE OF DEATH

By

BellaDonna Drakul

Chapter I

Life's beautiful images can never be seen until death manifests and all becomes clear in the light of day. If that is true, it is the highly deranged sights underneath that become less evident as compared to those that are more flattering on the surface. Alas, not everything in life is what it appears to be, as one might believe. Some pictures are disguised as visions of loveliness to the naked eye, secretly running rampant with chaos to those who seek wickedness. And in a world where diabolical paintings are hidden from normal view, those who do not hide beneath evil veils will never see what is perceived to be a vision too frightening for words. The innocent will only notice the elegant and graceful broad strokes and not the truer sight of ungodly streaks of horror. The colorful oils on the canvas seem gentle to the pure of heart, yet they are nothing more than suspected drops of blood, possibly created by a killer with low morals. They are seen as artificial crimson hues full of erotic intrigue, impending nightmares, and daring colors that we fear in the dark upon unseen pallets of despair. But whatever they may be in the eyes of others, they alone complete the dastardly painting eloquently designed by a monster beneath a man of sensual appeal…

Now I shall admit the aforementioned is a strange thought to conjure, but one only a tragic being, such as myself, would understand. Perhaps it is because I am a tortured soul that suffers in a mysterious realm of creativity that I know I will never escape from. Or it could be that I am an artist who starves in silence with a maniacal cluster of bewildering thoughts that haunt me to the point of insanity. A depraved creature who trembles with pain over the talent that he can never fully express to others.

Someone who will never know that real beauty can be if seen if placed from the right angle. But I must not fret over such heinousness, for all cannot be lost in ugliness when it comes to certain aspects of my life... at least not in the living version. That is another peculiar statement, yet one that I know will make more sense once explained in full detail. With that being uttered, I suppose now would be the appropriate time to tell a bizarre and magnificent tale that one would usually ignore, but will never forget. A melancholic narrative that one may never fully witness in the life of a mortal, but rather one that will be carried on for generations through the eyes of an immortal painter. And lastly, a story that will satiate your brain with questions of sadness only if you are internally vile. I suppose the beginning is always the best way to start as my tragedy quickly rouses on a chilly evening in a despicable lair where all is seldom beautiful in the eyes of the beholder.

3rd of October, 1777

I am a man with nothing left to give, a bastard who should not be alive when others are more deserving of such a blessing. I am a demon inside of an empty space that all see as unfit on this plane of existence we call Florence, Italy. An average man who others pass without a second glance or an offering of a small morsel. And, even though I see all around me as unjust, my paintings are more than likely the reason I am ignored. Yes, they are rather bland to gaze upon, even more so than I am, in actual reality. Such a tragic opinion of one's self to acknowledge, it saddens me no matter how truthful it is… Indeed, I am a poor artist whose work is so beyond horrid it will only truly be applauded centuries after my own death. That is if I am that fortunate by then. At this point in my depressing life, only a torturous suicide would be considered my "greatest work of art," but not even that would be enough. Or would it?

"Oh fortunate death maker… come speak to me in my lowest of days and grant me the serenity that I beg for nightly. Hold me close to you beneath the shadows and slay me promptly." My heart sighs with a metaphorical heaviness as if the beating within is pointless. Perhaps it is and I am too blind to see it. Alas, ever since I became the wretched artist that I am today, I have been ridiculed and shunned by my peers more times than I feel I deserve. I have been dubbed a failure in the eyes of the more experienced and have even been told by those same individuals that I'm nothing more than a pitiful mistake in society. "Is it true what they speak of, dearest death maker? Would it indeed be better if my body was laid to rest in a monument of despair? Or are my words simple rambles from the brink of insanity that burdens me so?" I bellow out to the stars above me as a cluster of thin clouds roll past me without too much notice, praying my inquiries are answered sooner rather than later. But, as I wait for what seems like centuries, I find myself becoming more lost as time passes me by and I am left alone with my own selfish grief. Or am I truly unequalled? It seems to be the case as I find myself dancing inside of the beautifully macabre English Cemetery of Florence with an essence of death breathing hard down the nape of my neck from behind not nearly an inch away. Almost as if I wasn't as alone as I assumed... "Good evening? Is someone there?" My heart beat even faster than before in my chest as the pungent stench of death blew around me, shivers running down my spine. "Are... are you human? If you are, answer me now!" I shrieked with an obviously frightened tone within my speech.

"You must not think such oddities of negativity, Monsieur Xiomar, and I suppose it depends on what you consider human as to whether or not I will reply to your petrified series of inquiries," huffed a vehement voice of a stranger, baring the obvious tone that he was indeed of the breathing breed of mortals. Or was he? I was rather intrigued by the intellectual tone protruding from the man who stood behind me, yet I was too afraid to gaze upon him, for I knew he wanted to make his presence a brief mystery.

"Who…who are you, unknown gentleman? And how… how do you know my identity?" I sighed with terror laced into my vocal chords while shuddering profusely as to how he would reply.

"Who do you want me to be, Monsieur Xiomar?" swooned the soothing individual, or what I assumed was such, into my ear. The being's tone was oddly erotic and it would have melted a stick of butter if it were present. I was still too frightened to face him. "Am I not all that you asked for? A being to seal your fate and carry you into the next life, yes?" He cooed, breathed heavily, and thrust his fingers viciously into my hair. The bony digits of his hand grasped tighter as he spoke and I in turn was speechless for the moment. "You asked for me to be here, yes?"

I nearly vomited in my mouth once I was able to compose myself to answer his inquiry, for I already knew who he was before I saw his face. "It… it is you, yes? You are my death dealer, are you not?" I gasped and anxiously awaited his response as the air grew thick with anger all around us in a cemetery that was radiant and nearly as old as time itself. A place of purity and peace that the living had forgotten, but one that I ventured to nightly searching for someone resembling this particular mysterious man. "I am, Monsieur Xiomar… or for less formal purposes,

Monsieur Drago. Which title would you feel more comfortable with?" And before I could tell him that only my school masters dubbed me by Xiomar, I turned to relish on the sinfully terrifying vision of a well-dressed gentlemen in garments of black velvet and crimson silk who carried a silver cane of pure elegance. My mouth instantly became dry, even though I knew the being was living, and remained still until he uttered another statement.

"I believe I shall call you Drago, for if I am to make you mine, then all ceremonious titles should be dismissed. Wouldn't you agree?" The severely boisterous wind from the bleak autumn evening became more odorous and frigid as the unknown individual stared deep into my eyes with reflective white spheres that were neither good nor evil. No, they were more on the level of empty than anything else, as I sensed that he was attempting to hypnotize me with them. "Are you still of sound mind, Monsieur Drago? Or has the very sight of my appearance left your mouth without even a minute phrase to pronounce aloud?" He chuckled with a sinfulness that was neither horrid nor cheerful; a mixture of both, in a sense.

"I suppose so…" I said with a sliver of hesitation as his eyes appeared more startling to me, so much so that I had trouble regaining my thoughts. "But back to the matter at hand, what shall I call you? You have not even spoken of a moniker or anything else for me to address you as." I waited patiently for him to speak, but not for too long, as he then spoke rather abruptly.

"I do not believe we should bother with such miniscule details of one's life… but if you must address me as something, you may call me Monsieur Agostino. I am indeed a majestic gentleman, as the name implies," the eloquent man said while smirking at me with what I feared was something devilish. "So since all of the formalities of frivolous monikers have been laid to rest, I assume we shall proceed with the mildly grotesque subject at hand." My mouth became more withered at that exclamation as his obscure fingers graced my cheek in a tribadistic fashion, oddly causing me to swoon in a titillating tone. "Are you ready to meet your maker? To forget all that you have learned as a mortal and awaken to a life that dreads the very thought of your existence? To feast upon the weak and succumb to a realm of immortality?"

"There are far too many questions for one to decipher, Monsieur Agostino, but I am indeed ready to die. Unfortunately, I am not fully sure why I want it so..." Intense nausea rose within my throat as the concept of what he was instantly became evident as he exposed a smile that was brighter and more hostile than the moon that hung above us. His elongated teeth sprang forth almost instantly, uncontrollable fear becoming apparent on my brow, as he hissed psychotically towards me.

"My God... you are a..." And before I was even able to utter the identity of what stood before me, the bastard clutched onto my neck with such rage that I could barely breathe as he immediately tore into my flesh like a deranged beast from the wild. I felt my eyes flutter rapidly, nearly seizing in convulsions, as his teeth were like miniscule razorblades that seemed to impale me as if he was a child of the night as my mind told me he was. My blood gushed into his mouth rapidly and violently brought on dizzying spells that I could not ignore. Sadly, I knew that my death was coming sooner than I had planned and as much as I ached for it previously, I was not as accepting as I originally thought...

Chapter II

All is not what it seems once a man is willing to turn his back on mortality and become the monster he once feared. He has ultimately signed a contract with his own personal devil for an existence in a bloodthirsty hell where all is not as glorious as he dreamt. And when that particular being has become a creature of the night, he has indeed become something that shall never die. So if that is true, then is a lifetime full of death and destruction worth having just to ignore one of mortal nothingness? Can one's life truly be that ghastly to where they would trade it all for that of a savage killer who feeds off of blood to survive? When I was more youthful, I never believed it to be so until I was willing to succumb to that diabolical fate five years ago just to destroy my bland life as an unsuccessful artist. I was soon tortured by a creature that preyed on the living night after night and I let him take me into his realm of death. Alas, it was all just a poor excuse to escape who I was, yet it wasn't enough. Such a heinous action to undergo for an extension on my life, but it seemed to be my only option at the time. Was I wrong for choosing such a thing for all eternity? Unfortunately, as the years passed by faster than seconds, my answer became clear and I realized it was more of a curse than a blessing, for I am still seen as mediocre in the eyes of my more creative peers.

Yes, dearest reader, I had become quite selfish at the ripe old age of twenty-three and decided to "sell" my soul to a vicious blood-lusting fiend who not only robbed me of my life force, but my innocence as well. Sadly, before I knew what a true vampire was, I had already drunk the purities from several unfortunate fools who passed me by and I was left with nothing but regret over what I had done to them. Their blood kept me alive, but it aged me terribly and left me feeling like an empty shell with no reflection of my youth. For years, I found myself relishing on the crimson nectar of virgins, the elderly, and even the severely destitute and, no matter how much I fed from them, I still never felt satisfied. There was always a hollow feeling buried deep within my veins that occasionally awoke and when it did, it reminded me that there was no amount of blood that would ever happily fulfill me like being a successful artist would. That alone was my greatest dream and as time flew by, it appeared as though it would never be factual. There was nothing I wanted more and I was willing to trade my mortal years for those of immortality just to be something memorable. Was I deserving of such greatness? Is slaying others for survival worth doing every night just to no longer live a wretched mortal existence? At this time of my tale, it has been pointless altogether and I am starting to believe that I should have killed myself instead. For if you ache for a life filled with everything your heart desires and it doesn't come to be, you have wasted it all away like a distant memory in one's dreams. Or have you? Perhaps there is more to this plane of existence than I am seeing and my succession is closer to becoming real. That could be a realization if I beckon it... or it might be simple wishful thinking.

4th of October, 1782

The darkness has been brought on once again by devious-looking clouds over Florence. I am shrouded like a blanket in its obscurity as I hide beneath it all inside of a small area built on top of an unknown opera house. Oh, the music that bellows through my quaint lair is so enchanting... it is the only solace I can call upon in this cruel world. Classical music created by violins and radiant clarinets are quite brilliant to hear nightly and often lull me to sleep when the sun rises for the day. There is a remarkable essence in this place and there could never be an ounce of dread. And as wonderful as it all is, I am horribly lonely without a passionate love or glorious painting to call my own. It is an existence that seems to worsen as the days pass, but as I write this, I am immediately caught off guard by an angelic songstress that has entered the opera down below. "Oh, my..." I blink sporadically as her barebacked splendor has instantly caught my fancy and has caused my heart to flutter. "I must know her..." I cooed, straightening my sage-colored waistcoat while thinking of her. I decided to follow her to her appointed destination. Where it might be, I did not know, but I had to meet this woman or die trying.

Soon after, as I rushed down a spiral staircase to the raven-haired seductress, I couldn't help but wonder if she were a goddess in the garments of a ragged slave girl. She was rather divine and I yearned to paint her... and perhaps feed from her delectable veins. What I wouldn't give to taste her loveliness! Unfortunately, as soon as I had the chance to come to her, she quickly became startled and slapped my face after she turned to see me rushing towards her. "I beg your pardon, you sadistic fiend! How dare you approach a lady of my stature and in such an unruly manner, you diseased little man!"

"My apologies, madam… but I saw you from my quarters up above." I pointed to my small lair for her to peer upon. "And once I saw you, I knew I had to paint you, for you are utterly ravishing!" The youthful lady of nearly eighteen years old batted her lashes with a newfound flattery at me and instantly agreed to my artistic advancements. I must admit I was surprised that she united with such a statement so rapidly, but I partially assumed it was my vampiric attributes that might have persuaded her. Minutes later, I led the dark-haired maiden to my cluttered art studio, motioned for her to sit on a nearby chaise, which she happily accepted, and received a small satchel of gold coins as payment for my painting. "Thank you kindly, madam, for your cooperation, but before I begin, I would enjoy the delightfulness of receiving your name. Will you bless me with such?"

The girl blushed, her cheeks pulsating with fresh blood underneath, and whispered softly while brushing away an ebony tendril. "My elders dubbed me as Lunetta Silvio, which roughly translates to…"

"Little Silver Moon, yes?" I smiled, trying my best to hide my slight protruding fangs from her view, as she nodded at me and I gave her my name in return. "Now that we know each other well enough to at least be friends, may I paint you?" She gave her permission once more, dropping her lavender robe to the floor to display her elegant form, and I winced at what came next out of my mouth. "Oh, dear… it seems as though I have used my last canvas for an oil painting. What am I to do now?"

"You despicable fool! I should have known you couldn't afford to paint me! You disgust me and should never be dubbed a painter! I am leaving this pungent hole you call a home! Good day!" The maiden spat in my direction, began to cover her flawless backside with her robe, and that's when I noticed something more glorious upon her that I had never seen before. There, hidden in a fleshy mound covering her pale back, was an image of a tortured maiden surrounded by thorns that swallowed her whole. It was the most magnificent picture I had ever gazed upon and I ached to recreate it on something even as small as a scrap of parchment.

"Madam, do not be so quick to leave... I will give anything in this world to you if you allow me to reprint the breathtaking masterpiece on your back. I beg of you, I would be honored!" I hissed and pleaded with the woman, who burst with rage as she spoke.

"Are you quite mad, Monsieur Xiomar? There is nothing on my back... it is as vacant as your brain! Now if you please, I must leave in a hurry!" She screeched and bolted towards the small door of my quarters, but not before I realized what was occurring and ceased her actions with a violent nudge to the ground. She whimpered and fell on her stomach as the picture of an unhappy woman became more visible on her body.

Yes, there was indeed an image on that girl's back, but it was something that could never be seen by the eyes of a mortal. It was, in fact, a vision that only an immortal, such as myself and others like me, could witness and was far too brilliant to ever be noticed by anyone less than someone of my kind. As you will soon realize, there are some visualizations in this world that only a vampire will ever witness and as soon as I saw Lunetta's, I knew I would be rather wealthy very soon if I was willing to paint it for all to see. But without any paper to paint it on, what was I to do? And then my "paper" appeared right in front of me... the fleshy canvas known as her back. "Oh, my dearest Lunetta, you will be my greatest masterpiece ever!" I shrieked hysterically and what came afterwards in a hazy memory, which might have possibly been a bizarre nightmare, was something that can only be described as sadistically maniacal...

My mind burst into a metaphorical cloud of rage as I caught myself reaching for a nearby oversized blade and savagely slicing the maiden's skin from off of her back with one precise cut. "You sick... sick bastard! What... what are you doing? You... you will not get away with this... I won't let you!" She wailed neurotically into the air, my minuscule-sized body straddled on top of her porcelain form to keep her from moving, as I properly removed the large piece from her body and placed it gently off to the side. And while her deafening screams might have been enough to distract most individuals, I could not help but ignore it all as I was soothed by the lapping from my tongue upon her blood and the melancholic voice of the opera singer downstairs. Lunetta's blood spewed all around, bubbling in sultry puddles onto the soiled floor below, and made my heart pulsate with ecstasy, knowing that she was dying a beautiful death by my own hands. Once she stopped quaking with unbridled pain, I mustered the strength to bind her body to the chaise on which she previously sat, and forced her to watch me trace the intricate lines of the twisted woman that once graced her back that no mortal being would see otherwise. My God... it was all too enchanting to behold and, the more she screeched, the opera cries growing more intense in the background, the more I knew she would be my most wonderful painting of all and I would have no regrets.

"Oh, glorious Lunetta... you will be immortalized forever as a living work of art and there is nobody in this vile world that can ever steal that glory from you. I will make you perfect evermore..." I wickedly cackled and breathed new life into this maiden's once flawless form, making it into something that would be adored for ages, displaying each detail to its full potential with decaying oil paints. "And from this day forward, my lovely maiden, I shall be a true immortal artist!"

Chapter III

Once a gracious gentleman has become a devious bastard, there is not much that can be done to reverse his hatred. For if this type of incident has already occurred, you can guarantee that man is eventually going to bring chaos to all he sees fit and disturbing deaths shall rule the land. In due time, blood will swallow the paths of all it passes, the depraved shall rape and slaughter the pure, and there will never be a god for us to worship. All will be lost... all shall cease to be. However, as with everything in life, not all hope has vanished...

except for in my world. Yes, I would like to tell you I found my peace after I created Lunetta's haunting design entitled, "Torturous Tangle," but then my tale of twisted thoughts and heinous actions wouldn't be as interesting. In fact, I would slay myself if I considered a lifetime of blissfulness achieved with only one painting bringing me wealth. I would be penniless and boring, which would prematurely force me to end my reign of terror upon Florence, and I am not going to let that happen! Fortunately, as I further my devilish details of my livelihood to my dearest followers, I shall continue by saying I was not as successful as I dreamt I would be, so I proceeded to share my "original" paintings with others of my caliber. Needless to say, I became obscenely wealthy over the next five years and nothing would ever change that. At least that's what I believed was true…

The following years were indeed hospitable to me after darling Lunetta died, for my thoughts had altered to gory psychotic levels and my pathetic feasts on mortals grew to sickening lengths. It was beyond perfection for an immortal who craves it all like I do. Alas, I had given into a realm of malevolent beasts adorned in garments of inferior royalty that soon followed me around as if I were a regal king. They craved my paintings, created with human flesh stretched across wooden frames with hellishly brilliant pictures depicting hidden truths, and practically praised me with a fortune that caused me to gush. And what made it worse was how they yearned for them almost as if they sensed the blood was fresh and they needed to taste it... they were disgusting monsters that deserve to be idolized. So, shortly after my raven maiden was no more and time passed by, I devoured twelve mortals and made them infamous as well. Their putrid characterizations were seen by all that lived and visited Florence, mostly rich individuals who lusted for the most nauseating of all painted impressions. They came by the hundreds with gold in hand and, while I adored them all, their payments never pleased me, so I then slain anyone who I deemed worthy of being displayed as a permanent image. Momentarily over time, I was viewed as something marvelous in the art world and knew that if I hadn't killed so many individuals and drew them with my vampire eyes guiding me, I would be nothing. I relished in the envy and knew my feeding rituals had to increase if I wanted to be a legend, so I had to hunt yet again. Luckily for me, it was an activity that I was rather good at and it had been quite a while since I had quenched my thirst with a delectable nectar that only an immortal would love.

7th of October, 1787

When I was younger, I cried to taste something delicious before bedtime that my mother would bring to me as a well-deserved treat. But as an adult, what I ached for would probably not be a substance she would joyously deliver. Regrettably, I care not of any judgment, since I have turned my victims' flesh into art. In fact, I hardly care for anything except success and utter greed. I no longer paint for wealth… I do it for vile pleasures alone without a sliver of guilt. Everything I do is considered sinful and until I am punished for the depravities I have caused, I will cease my painting for no one! I can promise that I will thrive on this train leading towards ultimate achievement and never once regret any of it! And as I close this journalistic entry briefly without pen, I shall speak with a bulky gentleman about my latest male piece entitled "Lost Heathen."

"Monsieur Drago Xiomar, how delightful it is to finally make your acquaintance!"

exclaimed an abundantly portly male who towered over my unusually small frame. I was immediately intrigued by his proportions as he worshiped me further, soon finding myself questioning where his hidden masterpiece lied. It was severely distracting my brain and I found myself struggling to hear what he had to say as I looked on all visible parts of his body.

"It is a pleasure to meet you as well... May I ask your name so as to know you a bit better or to seem less awkward when we speak?" I bellowed above the crowd of art enthusiasts who engulfed my voice in a cloud of brassy tones.

"My name is that of a strong hero, Valente Gerodi, and I am a lover of your art, Monsieur. I am astonished by 'Lost Heathen' and would love to hear your theory on art! There is nothing in this world that will ever be as sensational as your paintings... what I wouldn't give to be one of your muses. It would be an honor in all aspects!"

"I suppose you could say my theory would simply be stated as, 'Each painting is a story of its own and, in some cases, it takes a lifetime to create such finesse.'" I grinned diabolically over my wicked pun, which caused Valente to smile. "So would you be honored?" I stared at him, his expression turning into one of fascination by what I said. He seemed seriously attracted to the idea and motioned for me to explain. "I would be rewarded with your presence as one of my subjects, Valente. That is, if you are willing to provide your attendance." I stood firmly and stared hard as the gentle giant curled his lips and nodded his head enthusiastically at my offer.

"There is no one in this world that is as superior as you who I would want to depict me in oil paints, not even the great Botticelli and he is colossal!" the ample man said and gestured for me to lead him off to my studio for what he explained as art in all its forms.

Nearly an hour after the moon shone brightly over Florence and the art show had ended with dignity, I traveled towards my lair of painted death and escorted Valente to my studio just above the opera. Yes, my studio... where death is created, painted, and sold with a trace of vampirism. And even though it was a smidgen too petite for my tastes, it was the best location for obstructing the howls of pain with the vociferous vocals of the opera singers. You might say it was a perfect place for a man with an immortal secret... "Welcome to my home away from home, Monsieur Gerodi... please make yourself comfortable." I gesticulated as he bowed with kindness and sat upon the same chaise lounge that my dearest Lunetta had once graced. "Would you care for a potable? A glass of my finest *vino*, perhaps?"

"That would be delicious, Monsieur, and I am looking forward to tasting it." I smirked politely away from his view, poured the bloody red wine into a dark glass, and handed it to the male who craved the attention of my painting abilities. "You do your pictures over certain body parts, yes?" I smiled to agree. "Then if that is so, I will remove my dress shirt to expose my upper half, for it is the least hideous of my features." The stocky man sighed, as if horribly ashamed of his unhealthy body, and removed his grotesque striped orange shirt. "I am ready, Monsieur... Is there anything I should do before you begin?" Valente smiled childishly as my eyes scanned thoroughly over his form for my perfect image and found it on his gluttonous stomach, overflowing over his beige trousers. It was a flawless depiction of what seemed to be two demons riding a carriage into fire and brimstone, something that delighted my fiendish fancies. I had to paint it immediately or else feel the pain of a majestic piece slip through my fingers!

"No, newfound friend; that will not be necessary." I shook my head, motioned for him to quickly drink his beverage, waited a brief moment for the tainted *vino* to be consumed, bound him to the chaise, and forcefully stabbed a massive blade into his paunchy abdomen without warning. Needless to say, the screams were hard for the regular opera vocalist to cover with her vocals, as the gentleman howled like a beast into the night. In fact, his echoes of unimaginable anguish were so intense that my vampiric ears became quite sore from the quaking pulsations. "There is no need to cause such a delirium of emotions... you're bound to draw attention from the opera enthusiasts downstairs. I am fairly sure they came to hear the lady of the house sing, rather than you screech like a deranged mental patient!" I playfully hissed at him and exposed my demonic teeth, which brought forth an obvious expression of sheer horror.

"You're... you're a creature of the night! My God... you're a..." And before Valente could openly voice that he knew I was a vampire, I ferociously plunged my fangs into his jugular while carefully slicing into his stomach with as much accuracy as possible. It was nearly impossible to perform both tasks simultaneously, but there was so much skin exposed, it was rather easy to accomplish. It was all too simple, at least with the capabilities that I possessed. "Why are you doing this? What... what have I done to deserve such a monstrous affliction upon my... my person?"

"You wanted to be one of my masterpieces, yes?" Valente wildly bobbed his head from blood loss, which I took as his permission. "And now you will be one for all time!" I believe hysteria had overcome me at this point, but I found not the urge to acknowledge it, for I no longer cared for the lives of others. As of now, I see all mortals as being at my disposal when it is convenient and if we lose a few, then it shall not be considered a problem. It is not my fault that I'm more creative than my immortal brethren. I say, why not enjoy such things as death?

"You... you will be crucified for your actions, Monsieur..." Valente breathed heavily as I sat nearby, dipping my paintbrush into a perfect pool of blood that had gathered in his navel. I felt it would add a more realistic texture to the demons and the brimstone. "Somebody will be searching for me... you will be punished for your heartless sins... you shall be judged for your crimes! People will find out and somebody will... come for me!" Valente choked loudly on his blood, spitting it out in small bursts often, and struggled as best as he could to speak his piece, but as his breathing grew shallow, I found myself humoring him over what he muttered.

"Yes…" I huffed with a noticeable tone of sarcasm. "I am almost certain someone will convict me for my crimes, but I can promise you this, Valente… they shall think nothing of my heinous actions once they peer upon my newest painted prize that I like to call 'Sebaceous Demon.' And trust me, my heavy friend, you shall be worshiped as a god by all those who envy you and there will be applause from all directions." I grinned with insanity upon my brow and continued painting my newest creation with joy.

Chapter IV

It is known that a man's way of thinking becomes more volatile once he transforms into a being that not even he recognizes in the mirror. And it is also believed that if that is factual, the male tends to slay anyone he sees as a threat, regardless of their kind demeanor.

All are seen as evil to him and become his enemy once he lays eyes upon them. Unfortunately, I knew I was beyond that point and I found myself feeling more euphoric than I have ever been before. I felt nothing but bliss once I committed those ungodly deaths and still cared not for what others thought. Actually, some may say I am diseased in the brain while others may disagree and say I am a genius. Some may even spout out a phrase accusing me of vampirism while others may assume I'm a saint. But whatever I am seen as by others, as long as my paintings sell, there is nothing anyone can say to hurt me ever again. I am a being who has turned the other cheek on the mortal society and, because of that, I feel as though my soul has left me as well. I am a heartless, bloodthirsty killer and have vowed to be nothing more than that. From this day forth, that is my promise to myself... I shall not be anything less than a true artist. I will kill anyone who crosses my path and I mean anybody! Even the most virtuous ladies shall not escape my wrathful hand, which is where my tale continues five years and twenty-seven slayings after Valente Gerodi became one of my greatest works of art.

13th of October, 1792

Blood shall outline all of the most radiant pieces of art worldwide and my work will never be an exception of that. Since that is true, or at least I feel it is, then my newest piece will be most spectacular. For you see, I have found a beloved treasure that has captured my heart with her perfections solely due to what she possesses internally. But before I tell you all who she is, I must explain how she came to be... Her name is Cerelia Donatella, who is indeed a beautiful fertile gift as her name describes, and I met her through an acquaintance who I suspect is a vampire. But that last part is beside the point. To relate back to Cerelia, she was indeed a darling creature with a child growing in her womb and from the first time I saw her at a museum, I knew that she was destined to be my newest creation. And about a month after we met and just as I was about to visit her in her home, I caught her standing in front of a doorway with her protruding stomach on display and was instantly mesmerized by the unborn child that jabbed at her from inside as if to escape. Her massive stomach was indeed glorious and the vision I saw on it was something I craved to paint, the darkened image of a fetus with demonic attributes. It was at that exact moment that I truly knew she was to be my muse, so I decided to approach her on the subject... or at least warn her about it before I sliced the skin from off her abdomen.

"Good evening, dearest Cerelia... I assume you are well today." I politely said, kissing the hand of the fair-haired beauty as she invited me into her regal abode.

"I am as well as can be expected, Monsieur Drago, but this wretched child has been rather spiteful today and acts as though he wants to erupt from my stomach. Perhaps I have a demon or bloodthirsty monster inside of me. I am ever so worried of what he will be like once he is born…" She chuckled sweetly at her comment as I pretended to agree despite that last part.

"It is a boy, yes?" Cerelia shrugged her shoulders as if she had no idea, but explained she assumed it was so in relation to how the fetus acted. "Well, whether it is an ornery boy or a cherub girl, I hope they are healthy." She smiled at me, offered me a bland potable, which I declined, and began to speak of her pregnancy, which I paused to ask her a favor. "I am beyond delighted that you are with child, which is why I want to paint you... would you be willing to be my next masterpiece?"

"Not only would I be willing, but I would be more than joyous to pose for such a talented soul! I must undress, yes?" I nodded as we then traveled back to my studio posthaste, where she removed her cobalt-colored dressing gown, clumsily dropped it to the floor, and delicately laid her motherly form on the chaise. "Is this what you wanted, Monsieur Drago?" she said and mildly covered her supple breasts with her hands and crossed her legs to shield her vagina from my view.

"As a matter of fact, it is, but would you mind drinking this first?" I handed her a dark glass with an unknown liquid inside, which she happily accepted. "It will decompress you more and make this experience a whole lot more interesting. Do you care to partake in the beverage I have offered? I am quite sure that the dear child will enjoy it." Cerelia giggled at my comment and gulped down the tainted beverage with no questions asked. Such an imbecilic lady she was...

Minutes later, the dense woman woke from a surprise blackout and screamed frantically once she realized she had been tied to the chaise. "What is happening to me? What are you doing to me, Monsieur Drago?" Cerelia frantically panicked and tried her best to untie the slightly frayed ropes upon her wrists, but due to her impregnated condition, it was no use.

"Whatever do you mean, my dearest childlike mother? I would never hurt you... at least not permanently, that is." I sadistically smiled, sat next to the youthful maiden, who shivered from the touch of my hand on her exposed thigh, and removed a large blade from off of a nearby table. "I promise this will not hurt as bad as you think... Are you currently on any form of blood thinning elixir?" I snarled and saw a look of devastating terror in Cerelia's eyes as I raised the blade above my head for suspense and playfully brought it towards her stomach. Once I put the fear of God into her, I drug the blade across her abdomen and violently begin skinning her alive.

"Stop... please stop this now! Please..." the pregnant maiden blubbered and while in the past I would have felt grief for her, I didn't even wince when she pleaded with me to spare her life. In fact, I hissed psychotically as I found myself humming to an imaginary tune brought on by her screams. It was all too poetic as the lady wailed profusely, still begging for me to spare her from death's cold hand. I ignored her completely thereafter as I seductively licked the excess blood from off of her newly detached skin. "You're... you're a monster! You should be hunted down for... your horrid actions!"

I couldn't help but smile a bit at her remarks, her blood now dripping onto the floor below around my bare feet. "How am I a monster, my dear? Is there truly anything wrong with filling one's body with the blood of others?" She gasped at that moment, as if she had figured out my immortal secret too, but I kept her from saying a word as I licked her blood-drenched exposed belly and strummed my fingers in a happy tune for her fetus to hear. "If I were indeed a monster, then would I sing to your dearest boy?" I chuckled and began to sing, "Hush, little baby, don't say a word... Drago's going to kill you a mockingbird!"

"You sick bastard... don't touch me! Don't you dare touch me... leave my baby alone!" Cerelia thrashed around on the chaise lounge, repeating this same phrase until I had no other option but to choke her. As soon as the thought occurred, I viciously placed my hands around her sylphlike neck and threatened her with an inch of her life.

"Now you listen to me, you rude little girl! If you make one more move, not only will I break your neck, thereby severing your spine, but I shall relish on your child's blood beforehand! Now are you going to be quiet and let me paint you?" The motherly maiden whimpered at that comment, but what surprised me was that she retorted with a threat of her own, speaking and acting as though she was possessed by the devil or one like him.

"They are coming for you, Monsieur Xiomar...They know what you have been doing and they are coming to seek revenge for your exposure of their kind..." At first, I wanted to slap the girl for trying to distract me with such trivial words, but then I realized exactly what she was talking about. My suspicion of her vampire friend was true! "The immortals know you are abusing the gift they have given you and exploiting their breed just to gain wealth and fame... they want to punish you, Monsieur, and will be coming for you soon!"

I cackled at the silly woman's scourge, but wondered how she knew about a vampire's gift of sight. Figuring she was spinning a web of lies, I called her bluff. "Is that so? Well, if there was indeed a cluster of immortals coming after me, then who leads this bloodthirsty clan? Do they have their own vampire god to worship?" I laughed wildly at her words, hovered over her bound body, and tried my best to make her whimper in fear. Unfortunately, she didn't budge like I thought she would, and replied with confidence.

"Laugh all you want, Monsieur Drago, because when Ignazio Ruggiero finds you, he will slay you for your greed like that of a mortal! He will bring his kinsmen with him and they shall not rest until you are punished severely!" Cerelia giggled like a demented doll, thrashing her body as if being electrocuted, until I sliced her fragile cheeks with my fingernails. Her blood quickly rushed to the surface, yet she shed not a tear from the pain I know she felt.

"And who, pray tell, is this supposed vampire, Ignazio Ruggiero? I have been an immortal for nearly twenty years and this is the first I have heard of him. He is fictional, yes?" I tightened the ropes around the maiden's wrists and yet again heard not a sound from her nor saw a kick from her unborn child. It was almost as if my devious behavior didn't bother her in the least, almost as if she was already dead before I could kill her.

"No... he is quite real, Monsieur, and if you continue this kind of indecency towards the mortals of the world," she paused as if to create a sense of suspense to her threat, "I will make sure he comes for you when you least expect it!" And once those few words were uttered, I spontaneously slit her throat with my blade to shut her up. It did the job, so to speak, but part of me felt melancholy for killing such a sweet jewel of a girl. Nevertheless… the feeling didn't last too long as I shrugged my shoulders afterwards and continued to create another mortal masterpiece entitled "Eternal Fetus."

Chapter V

It is within one's best judgment not to toy with a man who has been marked for death. It is especially not wise if it is a gentleman who has already been appointed to die once before. Many times, this type of circumstance arises when someone is buried alive, which is a "partial death," if you want to be strangely precise. But in other scenarios, this terminology is present for those who have chosen to walk through life as an immortal. And yes, my dearest reader, I am that man and I feel it is time to take a stand against those who want me to perish. I am, after all, a creature of the night. I kill individuals for survival and pleasure, I slay mortals for recreations considered art by the nouveau riche, and I drink blood often as if it was water. Why on Earth would I coward down against my own kind when a depraved human tells me I am to be hunted? I laugh at such exaggerated fables of mortal lore! In fact, I find the whole concept quite intriguing. I believe it to be ludicrous in all forms and I know that if I were on the extended list of vampires chosen to die, I wouldn't still be here. As I wrote in my journal long ago, that Donatella maiden was spinning a web of lies, but I was not willing to be her prey. No, I was far too ingenious for that, hence one of the many reasons I killed her over five years ago... Yes, more time has passed and many other humans have been slain for my own delight. Last I counted, it was seventeen more, due to my sliver of paranoia kicking in because of the possible vampire allegiance coming for me, but the number continues to rise as I am about to become a true legend at my largest art gathering to date at The Palazzo Vecchio.

31ˢᵗ of October, 1797

Tonight is the night where a mere hideous painter becomes a marvelous one and is finally going to be treated like royalty. And, the best part of it all was I barely had to suffer to get here… but my victims are another story. Do I feel remorse for the possible hundreds of humans I devoured and mistreated for my own personal uses? Or better yet, should I grieve over those who were angelic and sweet who gave me no reason at all for killing them? No, on both accounts, and I will not let them or anyone else in this world keep me from obtaining my prize! I have suffered greatly and now I believe it is time for others to feel the torture I have dealt with for far too long. I believe it is not wrong to feel this way. For if you are an immortal, nothing is seen as immoral when humans are involved. And now that I have said that, I am currently being approached by a true pure-hearted mortal known as Madam Kathalina Quorra. She is an elderly lady of elegance who unfortunately is too thin to skin for my masterpieces, hence her life being spared. She should consider herself quite fortunate.

"*Buona sera*, Monsieur Xiomar, it is truly an honor to have your show at my galleria! You must be proud of your achievements, *si*?" The mildly fluent Italian woman uttered and curtsied towards me as if I were indeed royalty. I found it peculiar because she was the one who was more reserved than I was and should be treated far better.

"Good evening to you as well, Madam Quorra, and I am rather gratified of my work… thank you for holding this event for me." I bowed towards her, but was interrupted once she changed her temper and handed me a golden-sealed envelope, pointing towards a well-dressed gentleman across the room whose face was hidden behind a garish mask. "May I ask who this is from, Madam?"

"He would not say his full name, but I think he prefers to be dubbed Monsieur Agostino. He said you would remember him if he told you his moniker..." And as soon as she said that regal name, I knew that my master would save me if there was an actual vampire tribe coming for me. He would spare me from these fiends, yes? He was, after all, my maker, so why wouldn't he? I did not know why I was thinking such trivial thoughts, but the paranoia had fully set in as I carefully strolled over to speak with a male who claimed to be my vampiric maker... or at least I hoped he was.

"*Buona sera*, Monsieur..." I held out my hand towards the masked man and waited for him to extend his hand in acceptance, but not before I whispered, "Or should I say Monsieur Agostino instead?" I simpered in his direction as he returned the expression and replied with a phrase that froze my stance completely.

"You could address me as such, Monsieur Xiomar, or you could call me by my actual name... Monsieur Ignazio Ruggiero." My heart skipped a beat as the disguised gentleman grasped tight on my hand, forcefully pulled me towards him, and whispered into my ear with a sinister tone, "You selfish bastard... you not only made a mistake by exploiting the immortals with the gift we gave you, but you also broke my heart when you slew my dearest niece, Cerelia, and her infant son." He briefly paused and tightened his grasp as I struggled to free myself from his clutches. "For those deceitful betrayals, your immortal kinsmen are going to treat you in the same despicable manner that you displayed upon others. Consider yourself warned..." The maniacal kindred hissed and, before I knew it, he had gestured for a cluster of at least twenty immortals with the words. "Now you must do to him what he has done to others..." My master chuckled devilishly and before I knew it, I was stripped completely naked by a horde of vampires in front of my artistic peers, who boisterously laughed at my expense. Once I discovered what was going to take place thereafter, I ignored my own public humiliation and attempted to run from the current scenario. But much to my surprise, my maker knew how I would react and again motioned for his men to grab me and pin me to the marble-covered floor. "Where do you think you're going, Monsieur Xiomar? I thought your dream was to be held on a pedestal by your followers, was it not?"

"Why are you doing this, master? What... what are you going to do to me? I meant no wrong..." Before I continue, I need to explain everything I just said. I knew exactly what was going to happen to me, I knew why I was being punished, and I felt no guilt for what I had done to any of my victims. So why would I display myself as a merciful man instead of the loathsome one that I actually was? Why would a depraved individual confess what he really was? That alone would prove I was truly insane and I was going to take my punishment in full. But until that time came, I was going to plead innocent with the hopes that my peers would stand up for me.

"Do you really believe these mortals can't see what you are, Drago Xiomar? They know you are a savage killer and they know that you have slain their mortal kinsmen more than a true vampire should. After all, did you not think it was strange that your gallery opening was on a night where all evil comes out to play?" I gasped at his remark, but as the stares around the room altered from human to those of vampires, I knew that this was not going to be a hospitable gathering by any means. "As a matter of fact, you may not recognize them, but a large portion of the patrons tonight are descendants of your victims… and they are here to penalize you properly. Ladies and gentleman," the room filled with hisses and snarls in my direction, "you know what to do…"

I felt the hatred within the museum swell as my eyes peered upon the room's inhabitants, watching them remove elongated blades and knives from their pockets and satchels, and knew if I didn't confess to my sins now that I would surely become like the mortals I skinned for twenty years straight. "Cease your actions!" I howled as the crowd surprisingly halted, briefly holding back their weapons, as I knew this was my only opportunity to speak, so I gave a speech that not even the vilest being could ignore. "I admit that what I did was horrid and I can never be forgiven for that. But can you not forgive someone who only ached to complete his life's dream? A man who gave

132

up his very mortal existence to become something better? Doesn't that mean he should be spared and given a second chance?" The group of potential killers grew strangely silent and that made me think that they understood my pain and knew I was only living my life to the fullest.

However, after I pleaded my case, I suspected that my last words should not have been so selfish... "You pitiful excuse for a vampire! For that ridiculous speech alone, you shall be fully punished and become that which you create for others... kill him, kill him now!" Monsieur Ignazio wailed as the seemingly kind crowd followed the orders of their leader and rushed towards me with blades and fangs bared. And before I could pronounce another outcry, I was ripped to shreds by those I believed were my allies with barbaric tools of destruction and jagged teeth that could tear through the thickest flesh in one bite.

Suddenly, as if by some sort of bewildering nightmare playing in reality, I personally witnessed my pale skin being torn from my small frame and discarded across the room. I instantly howled vociferously into the air and couldn't stop what I sensed would take a small matter of time to complete. The scratching sound of ripping flesh was remarkably heinous, but not nearly as putrid as the actual visualization and pain I bore as I continued to be thrashed apart like those from my past. My blood splattered on the walls, my skin landed on the soiled floors below, and chunks of my internal organs were carelessly tossed in front of me. I then screeched like a banshee as the demons continued the prehistoric war upon my body by leaving me with nothing more than a head and torso… a macabre sight to witness for any sane individual. It was indeed a cruel fate for a supposed gentleman, but seeing as how I was a diseased killer as others saw me, I knew that what took place at that moment was justified on all accounts. It was true, I was a monster like Cerelia had said and, because of that, I was now enduring the exquisite pain that they all felt and I feared that I would become what they ended their lives as... a living masterpiece.

"My fellow immortals, we must now reap what he sowed and bless him with a gift that he never saw coming. This perverse bastard shall now feel the agony he brought forth to others for far too long... you know what to do!" Monsieur Ignazio cackled loudly and, just as I suspected by the phrase he spouted, the horde of artistic vampires huddled around me and began stretching my skin onto wooden canvas frames. They then proceeded by withdrawing harshly designed paintbrushes from their pockets for the creation of a masterpiece of diabolical attributes from my disposed body, disgusting images being crudely traced for future generations to enjoy. A tragic and just ending for a being that truly deserved it and one that will become part of our history for all time. So now, if you have read my tale and sense that this is my ending, then you would be entirely mislead. For you see, anything can be considered art but a true masterpiece, even if it is from a deceased being, shall live on forever and I, dearest reader, am eternal proof of that...

About the Author

BellaDonna Drakul is an international horror novelist and vampirologist from Tulsa, Oklahoma. Dubbed as "the next Anne Rice," BellaDonna is an active member of the horror community, with such famous fans as Stephen King; Sid Haig (Captain Spaulding from "House Of 1,000 Corpses"); Courtney Gaines (Malachi from "Children Of The Corn"); Lucky McKee (director of "May"); and James O' Barr (creator of "The Crow"), and is currently working on her sixth and newest novel, *A Stroke Of Death.* Her five book vampire series, *The Drakul Diaries* include:

The Vampire Collection: Short Stories for the Vampire Enthusiast

The Immortal Memoirs

The Kindred Confessions

The Undead Journals

Chronicles of the Ancients

THE MAKING OF MAREA

By

Scarlette D'Noire

Marea woke with a start. Her bronze body thrashed weakly about the bed, soaked from sweat and agitation. This had been her resting place for the last three days. Too weak to move, the chamber had become her tomb. She asked the same question of him in her island accent. "Is it finished?"

Not one to jump when called upon, Delano deliberately held back his words. He sat in the wing-backed chair, as regal as ever: perfectly straight, legs crossed, walking stick by his side, and his ever-present ring on his pinky. Impatient for a reply, she tried to rise from the bed, but fell weakened back onto the mattress. She yearned for the velvet tone of his voice to caress her ears and the soft kisses as he murmured words of love and lust in French.

"Please....tell me."

Delano rose from the chair at a snail's pace. Time slowed to a crawl. She watched each muscle of his body flex in his movements. The hair on his arms moved in the wind, something the human eyes ordinarily wouldn't see at such a distance. *How could this be! What is happening to me?* He undid the buttons on his shirt one by one, his slim fingers working downward in slow motion. His hands were soft, well manicured. *The hands of a gentleman.*

His muscles flexed as he removed his shirt, revealing a scar deep across his chest; the last memory he had as a human. The sound of the water crashing into the bathtub assaulted her ears.

"Turn it off! Please, the sound hurts my ears."

He ignored her request, running his long fingers through the warm water, sprinkling bath salts in to sweeten the smell. His agile body glided to the bed. Her eyes followed the lines of his toned physique, a slight treasure trail leading to the evidence of his desire. Marea breathed in his scent. Her sleek form responded. Craved him. The loud thump of his shoes hitting the floor further hurt her ears. "No! No! What is happening to me?"

"Calm yourself!" The sternness in his voice made her go rigid. Marea lowered her head. Softer now, he tried to soothe her, speaking in caressing tones. "Shhhhh, it is all right. Will the sound out of your mind. Concentrate. You have the control."

The volume in her head became quieter. She held her eyes down away from him, whispering in tones so soft only a vampire could hear.

"Is it finished?"

"Yes, my love, It is finished. Didn't you wish it to be?" Delano moved to the dressing table, gathering towels for their bath. Marea's throat tightened.

"You killed him!"

Delano did not answer. He walked toward her in a rhythmic pace, the anger in his veins rushing, coursing, moving, competing with his passion. He glanced down at the curve of her lips, the swell of her breasts. Yearning. Passion won over anger as he answered in a whispered rush.

"Your lover is dead. Extinguished. All he had is yours, my gift to you, beautiful Marea."

He brushed over her nipples as he untied the strings to her nightshirt. To his surprise, she began to cry; soft, low sobs. Dejected, Delano turned to leave, resentment slightly noticeable in his voice.

"If that is all you wish to know, then I will bid you a good night."

"No, please, you misunderstand."

He stopped in his tracks, weakened by this exotic girl. Delano had wanted to take her for so long. Too many nights, he had watched her. The plantation owner took her in as his wife. The thought of him touching Marea made his blood boil. He would have killed him weeks ago, but Marea would have been vulnerable as a slave girl without ownership of the Estate, a luxury she could possess in Florida, still under Spanish control.

"What is it I misunderstand? Your feelings for me or your sadness over your dead Master?"

Marea cried harder now. Delano never referred to her slave status.

"It is true, I was not free. Owned, like a dog. But he was a decent man. He allowed me into his home to sleep in his chambers. To live a life better than the others. He loved me. But you can set me free. Because of you, I am now master of my own house. To you, I am grateful, but I will never belong to anyone again."

Instinctively, he wanted to wipe her tears. Instead, he walked away. His vanity waned. In a rush, he turned toward her. At the side of the bed, he towered over her.

"You will always belong to me, Marea. If you like it or not!" He reached down, touching the back of her matted hair, pushing her down onto the bed. His body slid up between her legs, forcing them apart, the heat inviting him in. She willingly opened them, wrapping her legs around his back. Her matted gown stuck to his bare arms. He longed to be in the warm bath with Marea. Her skin, dark next to his, her firm long legs wrapped around his waist, her breasts touching his chest as she straddled his lap. He picked her up, walking toward the tub. She straddled Delano, waiting for this moment. He stepped into the bath, watching the bottom of her flimsy gown float above the water. The wet cloth clung to her breasts, her nipples visible through the fabric.

In his haste, Delano did not remove his pants, nor did he care. Transfixed, he lowered his head and bit into her breast, the warmth of her offering exploding in his mouth, caressing him, calling him to take more. Marea's head hung limp, her eyes rolled into the back of her head. He released her briefly, placing both hands on either side of her opened gown, ripping the fabric to her navel, exposing both of her breasts in their fullness.

"Are you ready, Marea?" His question was rhetorical. He would take her. Forever. Plain and simple.

"You have drunk of my blood for days now. Why do you think your senses are heightened? Are you ready to become what I am?"

She waivered. "I do not know."

Tracing over the sides of her curves, he worked his hands downward, ripping her gown completely open. She moaned, thrust forward, as Delano wrapped his arms around her silky skin and pulled her to him. Her nipples brushed his chest, sending waves of passion crashing through him. Kissing her neck, he fumbled with his pants, released himself, and entered her.

Hot white coal slid between her legs, greedily moving deeper into her. Her body, firm and lean, fit him like a glove. She met his thrusts with equal intent. Their bodies moved in unison, blended, intent on devouring pleasure. The contrast of their skin, fluid in motion, was beautiful and raw. Marea felt her resolve slip, weakened by Delano's touch. She kissed his lips, running her fingers through his hair.

"My love."

He possessed her for the moment, but that wasn't enough for him. "Are you ready, Marea? My patience is wearing thin."

Marea feigned uncertainty. For weeks, she had studied the incantations of her people, trying to find a way to become stronger than Delano and free from his grasp. She played his game to gain power and eternal life, pretending not to know what he was, all the while waiting for his fateful bite. Her lover, the Master of the house, had loved her - treated her well. But

Delano, greedy, full of lust, hatched a plan to rid the plantation of her Master. She would have it all. All except her freedom.

Delano thrust hard inside of her, causing her to rise slightly off his lap with each stroke of his hips. His dark hair reflected hues of auburn in the candlelight. Marea stared at his face. *So perfect.* He opened his eyes, the colors swirling in ecstasy. He had never turned a girl while making love. The fantasy danced in his head for weeks: ravaging Marea, taking her blood and her body. All for him, to possess her completely. Delano did not wait for her response any longer. He turned their bodies. Marea now rested on the tub's hard surface. He bit into his wrist, allowing his hand to hang, blood dripping in the water. The sexual tension at its peak, he leaned down and bit into her neck as his hips moved furiously. The rush knocked him backwards. He grabbed at her, pulling her body up toward him. He held her so tightly, she could barely breathe as he took her to the brink of death. Her blood raged through his veins, furious and fast. He thrust his wrist into her mouth, exploding in ecstasy. Marea drank greedily from him. Delano's head began to spin, the sound of his own heart beating loudly in his head. The banging grew louder and louder as Marea drained his dark force from his body.

Breaking away, he admonished her. "Do you wish to kill me?"

Liquid crimson dripped from her chin. Arching forward, she kissed his mouth, their blood offerings mixing together. The heat pulsed through them as one. Marea felt the strength surge through her veins.

One lean leg at a time, she exited the bath, dropping her gown to the floor. Her nakedness gave Delano the encouragement to find the strength to get out of the bath and remove his wet pants. Marea pulled the old sheets off the bed, exposing the bare mattress. Wrapping her damp body in the bedspread, she walked toward Delano, inviting him into the folds of the blanket. He wrapped his arms around her body and grabbed at the fullness of her backside. His strength returned quickly and he scooped her up, walking toward the bed.

"Are you feeling all right? The change shouldn't be as painful, since you have shared of my blood before."

She had been ready for this moment all her life. Pulling away from his embrace, she twirled about naked, laughing. "I am fine, Delano, but thirsty."

He laughed as he stretched out on the bed. "You have had enough to drink, my dear."

Marea walked toward the cabinet filled with liquor. "I want to celebrate."

She opened a bottle, pouring two glasses of whiskey. Behind the bottles of alcohol, tucked into the corner, lay a small vial. Marea opened it and drank the elixir without Delano's knowledge. Her hips caught his attention as they swayed back toward him. "Drink, my love. To life." She kissed his ear, snuggling next to him. Delano lay content. The King of the Jungle with his latest conquest. He wanted to rest, but Marea had different plans, climbing on top of him. She rubbed her nakedness against him in long even strokes, awakening his desire.

"Drink from me, Delano. I give myself to you."

Her wrist, close to his lips, smelled of jasmine from the bath. He breathed in her scent, clasping down hard, her blood offering flowing into his mouth.

"Yes, my love....Drink"

Slowly, she began to chant words that Delano did not understand. Lightness took him away. His eyes became heavy as he suckled her wrist, his grasp weakening until his mouth, now lax, dropped her wrist as he drifted off to sleep.

Two days passed before Delano woke. He tossed in the bed, groggy, unsure of his current situation. *Marea.*

Stretching his nakedness, he wrapped a towel around his waist, ready to make his way downstairs. Out of the corner of his eye, he spotted an envelope with his name written on the linen paper. The note inside read as follows.

My Evil Prince,

Thank you for the dark gift of eternal life. Although I am grateful for this gesture, I shall not be owned. Not by you or anyone else. Do not act willful in your sorrow or vengeful in your naiveté. As I am sure, scenarios of revenge already play in your head. Know that my secrets are many. My powers are strong. You will not find me. Yet, rest assured my love, if I desire too, I will find you. You have but a few days to leave this estate before the new landowners arrive.

Forever,

Marea

Waves of nausea gripped his stomach. Playing the evening back in his mind, Delano realized she had drugged him. *What the hell did she chant? Bitch!*

The house sat quiet except for one lone servant girl in the kitchen. Dressed only in a towel, Delano walked rapidly down the stairs.

"Mr. Durant, sir, are you ready for some supper?"

The girl walked from behind the counter, wiping her hands on the apron tied at her waist. Her eyes grew wide as she took in his near nakedness.

"Mr. Durant, sir, I, I shouldn't be seeing you unclothed. Sir."

She fidgeted nervously, unsure what to do next. Delano smiled at her embarrassment. The hunger hit. Ravenous, murderous, thoughts flooded his brain. The light scent of her fear and sweat filled the air, competing with the biscuits in the oven.

"Come here my love. Come to Delano."

She walked toward his outstretched arm, enthralled by his beauty. He cradled her in his arms and stroked her cheek.

"There, there. No need to worry, little one. You will tell Delano what he wishes...Yes?"

The servant girl, under seduction, nodded in agreement. "Very well, my love. Where is Mar-Ree- Aa?"

He said her name slowly and deliberately, pronouncing each syllable as if they were separate words, each dripping with his fury and desire. The girl succumbed to his charms, swooning in his arms.

"I cannot tell you the answer. She will not allow me to, sir."

Delano didn't understand how she could possess powers stronger than his, one made so new. *How can she control this girl?* Impatient, he took her face in his hands.

"Look at me closely. You desire to live and be free? Yes? Then you must tell me everything and forget Marea's instructions. Do you understand me? Your very life depends on your strict obedience to me."

The girl nodded. "I understand, Mr. Durant, sir. But I cannot tell you. I am to offer myself to you, sir. That is Marea's wish."

Furious, he tore into her neck, drinking savagely from her, draining her fast. Her young life over, he threw her down like a dirty rag. Disgusted, he broke everything in sight. *Marea! How could she keep the girl from revealing what she knew to me?*

The stillness of the house was deafening. The breeze, rustling through the Live Oaks, echoed in his ears. The young girl lay dead on the floor, her eyes transfixed in a glazed over stare. Slowly, he sat on the floor amid the rubble. He pulled the dead girl close to him. His fingers reached, touching the dead girl's hair. He twirled the ends around his finger over and over. The ominous stare from her cold, dead eyes gazed up at him. He lowered his head, staring into her eyes.

"How did she stop you from obeying me? How did she control you?"

Disgusted, he pushed her body away. The full force of Marea's betrayal stung his heart. It wasn't that he loved her or longed for her in that manner. No. Delano never truly loved anyone, especially not a human. Grand plans danced through his head. The scenario had played out often: how they would run the plantation, he Lord of the manor with Marea by his side. Plans that were now dust. He offered her freedom and, in return, he expected her loyalty. He couldn't help but feel rejected. The quietness of the house made his thoughts pound in his head.

Alone again.

Slowly, he began to rock as the tears fell.

About the Author

A lover of all things vampire, this is her first attempt at writing fiction. She is currently working on two books in the Vampire Historia, a Series of Revelations: *Nicolai's Fate* and *Delano's Undoing*. Originally from Chicago, she is an American author currently residing in Florida with her husband and two furry children. Scarlette D'Noire is a *nom de plume* used to protect the true identity of the author so she may bring Vampire Historia, a Series of Revelations to light without consequences.

ONE NIGHT WITH THE VAMPIRE

BY

Emily Walker

It all started over drinks one night with two of my employees. I can't say that I ever thought I would have a supernatural sexual experience. Once vampires made it known that they existed, it opened up a whole new opportunity for people to make money. The first businesses that popped up were "Take a Photo with a Vampire." They soon realized this wouldn't work because the vampire wouldn't show up in the picture, and what they were really selling was a picture of you posing awkwardly. The business men and women of the world had to get creative at this point and vampire escort services were born. Immediately, the vampires took over the businesses by simply telling the owners they no longer wanted them.

There were people who tried to get them shut down. They picketed all day and spoke out about sleeping with demons, but soon they realized their picketing fell on dead vampire ears. No one wanted to stay up past their bedtime to make a point, so the resistance dissipated for a while. The businesses operated for a while without issue; they popped up everywhere, kind of like those internet gambling places. The billboards were explicit, and no one could tell them to take them down because of their infernal mind-controlling abilities. The vampires were untouchable. Then, people started going missing.

Women and men alike would go to the escort services and never return home. Worried and very rich spouses hired private detectives and found out their loved ones had a dirty little secret. Once someone disappeared from the Horny Vampire or Vampires for Love, then they were never found. There was all kinds of speculation. Some said the police would just be mind-scrambled when they found the bodies and would just forget, while others said that the vampires simply ate the bodies after they killed them. For some masochists, this just made going to these places more exciting, but fear was struck into the hearts of those who weren't so keen on being offed during an experimental sexual experience.

So you are probably wondering how I, a twenty-four-year-old magazine owner, and successful business woman, found myself in the company of one of these escorts. I am almost embarrassed to tell you that it is because I lost a bet. My pride got the best of me, and I lost my head for a minute. Not only did I lose a bet so that I had to go into the escort service for a "fanging good time," but I also had to videotape it. I didn't have to videotape the naughtiest parts, but I had to prove I was there.

Drinks with two of my best ad salesmen took a strange turn as the night went on. I had taken them out to celebrate, landing a huge jewelry store as one of our advertisers.

"You two are amazing. How did you get Diana Della to agree to post her diamond pages in *Touché*? One of you had to have diddled her, right?" I truly believed that was how they had gotten the frigid bitch to agree with it. Todd and Bradley were young go-getters, and they were both easy on the eyes.

Bradley, who had been working for me longer, clutched his chest in mock horror. "I am offended, Bethany, that you would even suggest such a thing. I am also perplexed that a woman of your intelligence used the word 'diddled.'"

"Please, Bradley." I took a sip of my drink and watched as the two exchanged strange glances, solidifying my suspicions. "You two pigs. Well, however you got it done, cheers to a victory!"

As I clinked my glass with theirs, the topic shifted to landing the other diamond store, and stealing their ads from our rival, *Bette.* They had the same type of magazine and the men seemed to think taking their jewelry clients would be the best way to stay competitive.

"Even if you think you can get them from *Bette*, which I don't think you can, why would we want more jewelry ads?"

Bradley leaned forward and whispered, "Jewelry makes women horny."

"I don't agree with that statement at all." I said this, knowing I knew women who probably did get off on diamonds.

Todd grinned, wagging his finger at me. "Now, Bethany, you know it's true you get wet when you look at the assistant's engagement ring."

I was offended, but I wondered how the hell she had landed such a giant ring. She was my assistant and I knew what I paid her, and she dated a real estate agent.

"Fine. Women are gaga for jewelry. I still don't see why we have to steal them from *Bette*."

"It's the principle, Beth. They have it, and we want it, besides the fact that you don't believe we can do it gives me a hard-on to take that company and make them my bitch."

Bradley was so dramatic when he wanted to be.

Todd saw something towards the entrance and both of the men's attention spans were away from me. I looked over to see what they were staring at.

A blond woman without an ounce of fat on her and skin that hadn't been touched by the sun walked in. I was instantly jealous, wishing my drink was vodka and Diet Coke instead of vodka and Dr. Pepper.

"Vampire." Todd said it so quietly, I almost thought I had heard it wrong.

"No, her, really?" I hadn't been in the company of many vampires. I had to do a piece in the magazine on vampires in fashion, and had to meet with one or two at night. They were pretty stuck up – but this woman! She was breathtaking. I thought she was floating across the floor. It was eerie and beautiful at the same time.

Todd continued talking quietly. "I went to A Night with a Vampire last week. She was there in the room with me and another girl."

At this point, I spit my drink out all over Bradley, who looked disgustingly at me before urging Todd on. He wiped his clothes off the best he could with his hands. "Tell me what was it like? I have always wanted to go."

"They like to watch, dude, and they are totally freaky. I have never been with a kinkier woman than a vampire, and I have been with some crazy bitches. She can hear everything I am saying right now. Vampires have insanely good hearing." Within a flash, the beautiful blonde was in his face.

"Hello, darling. Maybe next time, you will ride me instead of Virginia." A long fingernail traced down the side of Todd's face and I felt like he almost looked frightened of her. She left him and walked across the bar and into a sea of people who were dancing. The bar we were at was upscale, but when everyone had too much to drink, they just started gyrating all over each other. Still the comfortable couches and amazing artwork were enough to keep me coming back.

"I couldn't see myself in one of those places, Todd. I am impressed that you have that sort of debauchery in you." I was impressed in a grossed-out sort of way, and not really surprised that Todd went through women.

"Do you really think we can't get that account?" Bradley signaled for another drink as he tipped his glass to get the last drop. The blonde had retreated to the bar, presumably scouting for some new prey.

"No, I don't think you can, I think it is pushing it after you landed Diana." I truly didn't think they could, which was why I agreed with what they said next.

"Let's have a bit of a wager, then. If we can do it, then you have to go experience a vampire escort." Todd was instantly intrigued and clapped his hands together.

"That's a brilliant plan. I know the perfect one." Of course Todd knew the perfect one. He probably frequented those places often.

"What the hell do I get if you can't get the client?" This sounded like a stupid bet, but I was almost completely certain they couldn't pull it off.

"A thousand dollars from each of us." That was a pretty sweet deal; they were both tight asses, so they must have been really confident. We shook on it and continued to order drinks until it was time to go home.

"You'll have to have some kind of proof, Bethany." Bradley leaned on a streetlight while we waited for cabs on the sidewalk. "A small camera. I will get you one. We will put it in your underwear."

Both men laughed and I shook my head quickly. I would not be making them their own personal porno. That was certainly crossing the line.

"I am not going to tape this, no way." I was mortified that he would even suggest such a thing.

"You don't have to tape the act; just going into the club and the guy before you do whatever it is you are going to do in that room, naughty girl." He jabbed me in the ribs like I was one of his buddies, causing me to glare at him.

We parted ways that evening and after I slept off the hangover that Saturday morning, I woke up pondering the bet I had agreed to. How many drinks had I downed without realizing it? I had never considered going to one of those places on a sober night.

Still, I went about my weekend hopeful, but Monday morning when I walked into my office, both Bradley and Todd were already there, waiting for me. As I hung my coat up, I eyed them suspiciously. What were they up to now?

"Good morning, boys." I smiled uneasily and sat down in the chair across from my desk. "What do I owe you, getting here earlier than normal?" Bradley especially was always at least an hour late, so the fact that he was here was not good for me. I had a good feeling I knew what they were going to say.

"You losing a bet." Todd smirked from his position, seated at the edge of the desk with his feet in the chairs I use for meetings. Bradley motioned me over to where he was sitting in my chair and turned the computer around so I could see it. I leaned forward, looking at the Mac's giant screen in disbelief.

Yesterday's blog for the magazine said that we welcomed Lane and Taylor as one of our newest advertisers, with a thrilled response beneath it from Mr. Taylor himself. Somehow, they had gotten to Cherie Lane. I was in shock. I should have been thrilled that we landed another big client, but this meant that I had to go through with my side of things.

"You worked on it over the weekend!" I couldn't believe it. I thought I would have the work week to change the bet, but no, they had gone out and made special trips on the weekend. They weren't really playing fair. I finally realized I was going to have to go through with this whole stupid plan.

"This was too good not to go after right away. I do my best work on the weekend." Todd wiggled his brows at me and I rolled my eyes. There was no doubt in my mind that Todd had diddled the Lane of the company. I didn't even see a reason to question him about it.

I tried to talk my way out of it when they insisted I go that night. Deciding I better get it over with soon, I told them I would give in to the night of vampire debauchery. I had no intention of sleeping with anyone. The camera on my shirt would show them just enough, then I would cut it off and leave. They could think whatever they wanted, and I would keep up the façade. It was a perfect plan, or so I thought.

So here I was in front of the vampire escort service, feeling dumb that I had let the stupid bet go as far as I had. The place looked like a normal bar from the outside, and aside from the sign that said *A Night with the Vampire* across the front, you wouldn't know any different. I turned back and forth so the small camera could see that I was indeed where I said I was going to be. How had I let two of my employees talk me into something this inappropriate? Looking back on it now, I think I wanted to be there. I used the bet as an excuse to entertain my curiosity.

Walking through the door, I was greeted by a supermodel clone of a vampire clad in a tight black bodice. Her breasts were spilling out the top, but remained perfectly round. She had on the tiniest pair of lace panties in the world. They were barely attached to garters holding up the most intricate pair of fishnet stockings I had ever seen. They looked like spiderwebs weaving in and out around her legs. I was distracted momentarily, giving her the wrong idea. She practically purred as she leaned forward and smiled at me.

"You are here for a woman sweetheart; I know the perfect one. She rubbed her hands up her body and over her breasts, looking me up and down. She licked her lips seductively, making me uneasy.

"No I actually am here for a man, please." That sounded ridiculous when I said it out loud, but it was the truth. I was nervous with this woman so close to me. As I had spoken, she had moved closer, and now wore a pout on her pretty little face. Briefly, I remembered she was dead with a mouth of sharp teeth, and shivered. The fact that I was surrounded by them was slowly starting to sink in as I looked around at the similarly dressed people all around me. Some were just sitting there, not blinking or moving, but I knew they were watching me.

"Right this way." She walked away from me, revealing that the tiniest panties in the world were actually the tiniest thong in the world. Such confidence these women had; I could never walk around in something like that. Of course, if my body wouldn't hold onto fat and I didn't have to eat, I might.

We went down a hallway with lots of rooms with sounds of pain and pleasure coming from certain ones. The cacophony of sounds almost distracted me enough for me to stop walking. I didn't, though, stumbling after her as her knee-high boots clicked over the floor. When we stopped at the very last one on the left, she said, "Here we are." She firmly grabbed my ass with both hands after pushing the door in. She walked me into the room this way, causing me to jump away from her. She growled at me as she went back out, and told me to get ready for the ride of my life.

Leaning against the door for a minute, I took deep breaths. They certainly didn't believe in personal space in this place. All I had to do was keep it cool and explain to him that I just wanted to be held. That sounded so lame in my head, but the decision was made. I sat down on the bed and tried to get comfortable. That was all that was in this particular room, a large bed with a red comforter and black pillows.

When I had gotten into the room, I had clipped the camera onto my bra. Once they saw the man and he whisked my bra off, there would be no way they could see what was happening. I had specifically asked that it be a camera without sound. No matter that I wasn't planning on having sex; I didn't want them to know that. If they heard a significant lack of moans, then they would be suspicious.

His voice came into the room long before he did; it was smooth and velvety. I was instantly on my feet and completely alert. Was he speaking through a microphone? Where was this creature? The words he spoke felt like they were traveling through my body, causing everything to heat up and tingle.

"Good evening. Take off your dress and turn around, please." I hesitated for a minute, not having planned for him to want me to undress immediately. I wasn't that proud of my body, and it was pretty bright in the room. There were no windows; just four solid walls. It sounded like he was right beside me, but there was no way he could see in the room.

I took off my dress slowly and laid it on the bed, feeling completely exposed in a simple lace bra and red panties. I had taken extra care with my underthings for a woman not planning on having sex. I didn't say anything, half expecting my next instructions to be delivered any minute. It was really quiet, and I felt like I had been standing in my underwear with my back to the door forever.

Finally, he spoke again. "Very nice, now turn around slowly and let me look at you." I did as he asked, feeling foolish as I turned all the way around and then stood facing the back wall again.

"Good girl. Patience is a virtue I like in my women."

I was shaking in anticipation, not knowing what to expect. My whole body was alive and responding to just the sound of his voice.

"I am going to show you a night of passion no mortal could ever give you." I felt his words throughout my being and felt all the heat in my body move to my core, preparing my deepest desire for him and him alone. This wasn't a good thing. Seeing as how I hadn't seen him yet, this reaction wasn't keeping it cool.

The door never opened, but suddenly, he was behind me. I could feel his presence against my skin, causing all the hairs on my body to stand up, even though he hadn't touched me yet. Swiftly, he disintegrated my bra, causing me to gasp in surprise as my breasts were suddenly exposed. His hands were now moving down my arms and, despite the cold feel of his skin, flames licked my skin wherever his hands moved. He ran them down my sides and grasped my hips, pulling my backside firmly against him. His body was rock hard, and so was his manhood. I still hadn't looked at him, but it didn't matter. He had undressed me so quickly and was pressed up against me so swiftly, I wasn't given time to look at him. I felt myself get wet at the thought of him taking me from behind without ever looking at him. This was not how I normally was, so the thoughts I was having were catching me off guard. I wondered if all the women were given this kind of experience when they came here.

Bringing one of my arms up to caress the side of his head, he moved to wrap both arms around my waist and spoke lowly in my ear. "Just relax, cherie. I want to make you feel good." The words, which would have sounded so cheesy from anyone else, made my whole being melt into his.

Completely lost in his arms, I had never wanted anything quite as badly as I wanted him, but I still resisted allowing him entry. This had gotten out of hand very quickly. I didn't even stop his hands when they moved over my breast, arching into him as he palmed them gently. I got the impression he was easing me into it. Extremely turned on and not in control of the lust moving through me, I considered the possibility of sleeping with him. That was what he was there for, and you couldn't catch anything from vampires because they didn't get sick. There was no way to get pregnant because they were dead and yet something about screwing a corpse should have stopped me. He didn't feel like a corpse, though. He was setting my body on fire.

Coming around to the front of me now, I finally got to look at him. He was beautiful with long black hair that had silver streaked through it. His eyes were yellow and his chest was fit, as was the rest of him. I was mesmerized by his beauty and intrigued by his unique appearance. Pulling me to him and wrapping my arms around his neck before moving them back down to firmly grasp my hips, his eyes bore into mine.

I was a goner. Only my underwear and his pants were between us now. Somehow, I found my voice. "You won't bite me, will you?"

Smiling and looking even more beautiful, he told me, "That's not part of the deal."

Finally, his lips found mine and his tongue pried my mouth open after tracing over it. I kissed him back hungrily, running my hands through his long hair. He was skilled with his mouth, and as his hands moved over my body, I was a willing slave to whatever he wanted to do to me.

My panties were tore away and he took off his pants. Without a word, he turned me with my back to him and bent me over, causing me to grab my ankles. He drove his hard, amazingly huge shaft into me, causing me to scream out at the shock of it. Standing there, allowing me to adjust to his size, he waited for just a moment before pulling all the way out and slamming into me again. This was something he repeated several more times before staying inside and pumping faster than a human could even think of doing. I couldn't tell if I was about to explode in ecstasy or if this was some delicious torture. I thought a couple of times that I was building up to a release, and he would pull out and plunge in again, disrupting the flow. Finally, I felt it coming deep within my belly, but just as quickly as my moaning started, he was out of me again.

Frustrated, I started to whine, when I was forced down onto my knees, my hands on the floor. He entered me again and dug his fingers into my hips, pulling me back and forth. It hurt my knees, but felt so good that I ignored the pain. Reaching around, he moved his finger over where he was pushing in and out, causing me to buck against him. His back was lying on mine as he filled me up completely and pumped hard, not taking his fingers away from my sensitive skin. Again, the orgasm was coming; I was so ready to let it go, my fingers digging into the hard floor, just praying for release. Of course it was some sick joke, like he knew when it was coming, because he pulled out of me again, laughing. How dare he laugh?

I was really starting to get frustrated when he sped forward, lifting me onto his shoulders and burying his face in between my thighs. I reached up to the ceiling for support as his tongue plunged in and out quickly. I held onto the back of his head with my other hand. He was amazing with his tongue, bringing me right to the brink, my whole body trembling, and then, without warning, he threw me down onto the bed.

Hovering over me, and I mean really hovering in the air, he looked down at me all that hair spilling into his face. I reached up and pushed it away.

"What do you want, Bethany?" He knew my name and it sounded good on his lips. I was extremely turned on.

"I want you to fuck me hard." The words shocked me; did that come out of my mouth? He drove into me again and I dug my nails into his back. I arched into him, wanting him to fill me completely and never leave. These types of thoughts scared me and excited me at the same time. His mouth found mine again and I bit his bottom lip. He growled, pressing his mouth into me harder and bringing both of my arms above my head, driving into me faster and faster, building me up again. I thought I would finally get to cum, but I should have known that I was completely wrong.

As soon as my body started to tighten up and shake, I felt him pull away, out and fly across the room, laughing.

"What the fuck!" I exclaimed despite myself. I couldn't help it; this was getting hard to handle. Feeling like my body was going to explode with need and desire, I was starting to get angry.

The laughing got louder as he came over to me, picking me up from the bed as I frowned at him. He was enjoying playing with me like this. I couldn't be mad for long, though, because he backed me up against the wall and started kissing my neck. He kissed all the way down the middle of my chest and to my belly button before moving back up and taking one of my breasts in his mouth. As his tongue flipped over the nipple, I felt his fangs for the first time. The feeling was indescribable. They shot pleasure through my breast that radiated throughout my whole body. I moaned loudly, wrapping my fingers into his hair and tugging.

He entered me again, pounding me against the wall as he continued to suck on my breasts. I felt the fangs pierce my skin and heard the low moan as his tongue moved over the small punctures. I realized he was tasting my blood. I was ashamed to admit that this turned me on even more. His thrusts got harder and he moved his mouth away from my breast, coming back up to my mouth and grazing my lip with his fangs. I moaned loudly and didn't even know what I was saying.

"Bite me." I was panting hard, building up to a powerful orgasm, and just decided I wanted his fangs inside me. It was a scary desire, but it was very real.

"That's not part of the deal." He spoke in a low voice never breaking his pace.

"I don't care. I will pay extra." Something was clearly wrong with me.

He continued thrusting hard and I felt spasms traveling through my whole body. Just as I was finally about to release and get some relief from the burning in my loins, he pulled out, dropped to his knees, and bit into the skin on the inside of my thigh dangerously close to my throbbing center. I screamed through the most intense orgasm I had ever had in my life, riding the waves and feeling like my knees were going to give way. He wasted no time pulling his fangs from me and bringing me to my knees. He slid his entire cock into my mouth, and pulled my head back and forth as I continued to ride the waves of passion and barely registered his fingers moving within me until I exploded into another screaming orgasm, causing his body to tighten and cold liquid to shoot down the back of my throat. Dear Lord, that was insane.

He lay with me on the floor, holding me for a little while. I felt like it was very intimate for a business arrangement. After he had kissed me sufficiently, he left the room, blowing one last kiss before disappearing and probably heading to his next conquest. I realized when I looked at my phone that he had given me exactly an hour of his time.

I walked out of the escort service, floating on air. No matter the thousands of dollars it apparently cost to get bitten. No wonder only the rich people were disappearing. Walking into my apartment, I was actually singing. I never sang, so I knew I was in a good mood. Wearing only a dress because my underwear had been completely destroyed, I had taken a cab, terrified the rain would show off everything I had. Otherwise, I would have walked the less than two miles to my apartment. Funny, I hadn't even realized there was a place like that so close to where I lived.

After the initial high of the evening wore off, I begin to feel a little dirty about the evening. There I was, prepared to trick the men into thinking I had done it, and I had actually done it. I had one night with the vampire, and liked it.

The worst part of the whole trip was no one believed me. Todd and Bradley said the camera never worked and they hadn't seen anything at all. They had decided I chickened out, and called it a loss on my part. I had the bite mark to prove it, but there was no way I would show it to them in the intimate place it was. I just had to eat their doubt and keep what happened that night between me and the silver-haired vampire.

About the Author

Emily Walker loves creating worlds and stumbling around in them. She writes under her name and the penname Lyra Mcken. She is constantly losing her chapstick, and has an obsession with the color pink. Currently a resident of the mountains and loving the view, she writes mostly paranormal fiction and horror. Her small family consists of her red bearded other half, a rat terrier named Rebel, and a cat called Mr. Creepy.

CODE BLOOD

An Excerpt

By

Kurt Kamm

During the thirty-minute drive to Hollywood, he thought he might be driving too fast, or maybe too slow. Markus wasn't sure which, but he didn't want one of the cops who patrolled Sunset Boulevard to stop him. He took a left off Sunset, making certain he used the turn signal, went down Highland, then turned left again down a dark residential street. Tucked away in an alley, Club Cyanide, or C2, as the regulars called it, didn't even register on a GPS. Markus drove slowly, looking for the entrance to the narrow cul-de-sac. He drove past it, hit the brakes, backed up, and turned into the alley. At the far end, he could see the glow of the small blue bulb over an unmarked door.

Markus parked in the darkness and slowly walked to the entrance. At the door, the security guard was busy on his cell phone. He recognized Markus and motioned him inside. It was early and the action didn't start until around one o'clock a.m. The club could be empty, but Markus didn't care. He didn't want to talk to anyone; he just wanted to find Marty.

Markus started up the steep stairs, grimacing at the pain in his back as he climbed. From above, he heard the beat, beat, beat of industrial Goth music and it made him feel better. Halfway up, the vibrations from the bass speakers shook the stairs. At the top, Markus paused and looked at the scene. There was a bigger crowd than he expected. In the low light, he watched the Goth crowd dance. People floated around the room. Couples rubbed their bodies together. Several men danced behind their women, with hairy hands cupping and squeezing their breasts.

Everyone wore black. The women had lace draped across their upper bodies. Some wore black feathers; others dressed in tight corsets and short black vinyl skirts. Mesh stockings and platform boots covered their legs. Black chokers, bondage belts, tattoos, and piercings were standard. Their eyes were black holes surrounded by heavy eye shadow and white face powder. The men were more simply dressed in tight black stretch jeans, black undershirts, and studded belts. In this group, Markus was an uber Goth. Even the most extreme makeup couldn't match his red eyes and natural white skin, hair, and eyelashes.

He moved slowly through the crowd and sucked in the atmosphere as an antidote to the noise of the Vicodin in his brain. He scanned the crowd for Marty, who always wore jeans, a black pullover and a sleeveless vest with dozens of pockets, each containing a different drug. Across the dance floor, Markus caught sight of a girl he thought he knew. Her real name was Alyssa or Alana; he couldn't remember which, but she called herself Goth Girl and everyone else called her Gigi. When he first arrived in Los Angeles, she let him crash at her place in Venice for three days. She looked heavier now and her hair was metallic blue instead of red. It was too dim to see the scars on her shoulders, but he was certain they were there. She was his first introduction to real blood play. She told him she was a member of Cirque de Sade and he thought he had finally met the right girl when she said, "Blood is the most erotic thing I can think of." On his first night with her, they stood naked in her bathroom and she cut tiny nicks on her shoulder with a razor. After the blood covered her skin, she pulled his face to her flesh and smeared the red liquid on his lips. The experience was new and exciting to Markus, something he had only dreamed about. After tasting her blood, he was in his own private ecstasy. He felt a rush he had never felt before, followed by an insane hard-on. They made love for the rest of the night. She threw him out two days later.

Markus wandered past the booths that lined the wall. In the shadows, he saw Marty, standing motionless, like a statue. Markus approached him. "Hey, Marty," he said.

The statue moved. "What's up, Markus? How come you're walking funny?"

"I hurt my back. Bad. I'm taking Vicodin, but it still hurts. I need something. Got any K?"

"Just picked up a batch from the vet in Tijuana." Marty fished in his vest pockets and pulled out a tiny plastic envelope with white powder. He handed it to Markus. "This'll help for a while."

"Thanks, man." Markus took the envelope and emptied the powder on the back of his hand. He closed one nostril with his finger and sucked the powder in through the other. "Ooh yeah," he said, as the Ketamine flooded his body with a warm feeling and increased his heart rate and blood pressure. For the first time since Grisha had kicked him, Markus felt some relief.

"It'll only last a couple of hours. I haven't got anything for long term."

"How about some X?"

"That won't do anything for pain."

"I know, but it might help me get through the next couple of days. I got a lot going on. I'll take a couple."

"Suit yourself." Marty fished out two Ecstasy capsules and handed them to Markus. "That do it?" he said, and scanned the crowd to determine if anyone was watching. "It's a hundred fifty."

"Listen, Marty," Markus said. "I have a problem. I need to borrow a grand."

"What?"

"I need to borrow a thousand dollars. You know I'll pay you back."

Marty glared at Markus. "I'm not a bank, asshole. No way am I lending you a penny. You owe me one fifty."

"Well, I haven't got it."

"Gimme back the X." Marty moved toward Markus. Marty wasn't much taller than Markus, but he was strong. When he wasn't dealing drugs, he was lifting weights.

"No." Markus stepped back and popped the two Ecstasy pills into his mouth.

"Damn you," Marty said, and grabbed Markus by the throat. "Pay me."

Markus shook loose and managed to swallow the pills. "Thanks for helping out a friend, Marty. I'll pay you next week."

"Friend? I'll beat the crap out of you if I you don't pay me."

"Get in line." Markus started toward the stairs leading up to the bondage play stations without looking back. He hoped Marty wasn't following him. By the time he reached the top of the stairs, Markus was beginning to sweat from the effect of the drugs.

There wasn't much bondage action going on. One girl was bent over, bound to the spanking station. Her skirt and black underwear were down around her knees. An older woman with fake dreadlocks of neon blue hair punished her with a short black leather riding crop. The concave-convex mirrors on the ceiling reflected back distorted images of the red welts on the slave's bare buttocks, which looked like flesh-colored beach balls.

The bare flesh reminded Markus of Audra. He imagined her at the Alley Kat. Some retard was caressing her elegant, long legs. She was bent over and the retard was doing her. She was enjoying it. She was crying out with pleasure. She was stuffing hundreds of dollars into her purse. Some of the bills were spilling out onto the floor, but she didn't bother to pick them up.

Markus tried to focus on the slave bound to the spanking station, but the China Doll bitch, Alexei, and Grisha were standing nearby, laughing at him. Marty came up the stairs and joined them. He whispered "Snowflake" to the others, and they all looked at Markus and laughed again. It was a conspiracy to make his life unbearable.

Markus fled the club. It was almost two o'clock a.m. when he walked outside. The light over the door was out. His head was spinning and the Ecstasy was surging through his bloodstream as he searched for his car.

About the Author

Code Blood has won several awards, including:

2012 International Book Awards; Fiction Cross Genre Category First Place

2012 NATIONAL INDIE EXCELLENCE BOOK AWARDS®; Faction (fiction based on fact)

The 2012 USA Best Book Awards; Fiction: Horror WINNER

LuckyCinda Publishing Contest 2013 FIRST PLACE; THRILLER.

Kurt Kamm lives in Malibu CA. He has used his contact with CalFire, Los Angeles County Fire Department, Ventura County Fire Department, and the ATF, as well as his experience in several devastating local wildfires to write fact-based firefighter mystery novels. He has attended classes at El Camino Fire Academy and trained in wildland firefighting, arson investigation, and hazardous materials response. He also is a graduate of the ATF Citizen's Academy

Each of his novels has a firefighter with a special skill: Wildland / Arson Investigation / Fire Paramedic / HazMat Specialist. Each mystery is told from the viewpoint of the firefighter and the story revolves around his specialty. He is currently working on his fifth novel, a USAR mystery.

His latest and fourth mystery - *Hazardous Material* – is now available. *Hazardous Material* recently won the Hackney Literary Award for Best Novel of the year.

www.kurtkamm.com

CONQUEST: MY VAMPIRE LOVER #1

(A Dark Realm Novella Series)

By

Victoria Embers

Author's Note: The first story, Conquest (My Vampire Lover #1) occurred AFTER Caroline was kidnapped and is told by Caroline, the heroine's point of view.

Caroline's Awakening

I didn't fight the urge to resist my lover when he came to me that night. There was a tingling sensation in the pit of my stomach that I couldn't deny. I wanted him now more than ever, despite our differences. I had grown to enjoy our nightly lovemaking over the many months of my imprisonment despite myself. I did not want to return to my family or my pack. They were all dead to me. I wanted to be with my vampire lover forever.

Without words, he removed my chains from my wrists and ankles. He had lined the cuffs with black fur, so the hard leather wouldn't cut my flesh. He tossed them into the corner and led me to the bed.

"Stay."

I nodded, standing at attention. Long ago, I had forgotten my embarrassment about being naked a lot of the time in his presence. I watched as he opened the curtains to the only window in the room.

When he secured the locks on the door and returned to stand before me, his naked chest rose to and fro in front of me. I could tell he was upset.

"They know where you are. We have to get you out of here."

"No. That can't be. They think I'm dead. How did they find me?"

"Some of our fang brethren have succumbed to your mother's charms, probably."

"Turn me. Turn me tonight," I pleaded.

"You don't know what you're saying."

"Yes, I do."

Gently he ran his fingers across the side of my face.

I leaned into his large hand, unable to resist the sexual magnetism that made him so confident for a vampire. My powers to fight him had steadily faded each night we made love. I raised my chin, exposing the contours of my vulnerable neck to him, knowing it would please him if I finally surrendered. "So be it," I muttered.

"Even if you survive, they will kill us if I turn you." His fingers laced around strands of my blonde hair as it cascaded over the contours of my firm breasts. He squeezed one of the nipples hard.

A low moan slipped past my lips. "We could leave this place," I whispered. "Together."

I immediately wrapped my hands around his cock. He was hard as steel, yet smooth as velvet. When he throbbed in my grasp, it sent me to my knees.

Slowly, I took him in my mouth as I placed my hands behind my back, offering my complete obedience. If it was to be my last night on Earth, I wanted it to be perfect. Surely the presence of the full moon would ensure a successful change. But a vampire turning a werewolf? Was it possible?

As I lavished the taste of him, moving up and down on his shaft, he spread his toned legs wider, slightly bending his knees.

I forced him further into my mouth, letting the tip of his head tickle the back of my throat. With each long stroke of my sucking, I devoured him whole-heartedly.

"You are eager tonight. Aren't you?" he asked as he pulled me up off my knees, holding me firmly in his masculine arms.

He shoved me into the bed and pinned my body against his. Letting his gaze penetrate mine, he stared at me and released his fangs.

A gasp escaped my lips. "Yes," I whispered.

He lowered his head and kissed the inside of my neck. Quickly, I felt the sharp edge of his fangs tracing the places where he had kissed me as his hands explored my breasts. Gently, he ran his fangs along the contours of my shoulders and chest.

Shivers of warm ecstasy rippled through me. *To be his forever.*

"Take me please," I demanded, glaring up at the ceiling. I slammed my arms into the bed, grabbing the satin sheets tightly in my grasp. I arched my back upwards to him. "I want to be with you forever."

"With all your heart?" he asked.

Wrenching my hands together, he held them before him. His eyes glowed, fierce.

The palms of my flesh grew numb and I froze. In his darkened bedroom where I spent my days alone and confined, I could only hear his threatening voice. Being with him every night was what I lived for. I longed to be his one true love. It didn't matter that I was different from him.

"Yes, I want to be yours forever." I pulled my body to his, forcing myself off the bed as difficult as it was to do. His hands bit into my wrists, but the pain didn't matter. "I'll forsake everything to be with you. Have I not proven that to you time and time again?"

"You have no idea what you're asking me to do. Drinking my blood is one thing, but turning you…" He released my hands and I sank down again into the soft bed.

Immediately, I felt his touch return. I closed my eyes, savoring the moment.

His touch was light and deliciously teasing. He spread my legs and took his time sliding his fingers down my stomach. Pausing at the entrance just above my sex, he ran a fingertip around the small triangle of hair. Then he slid two fingers inside me, instantly finding my clit with his thumb.

"You're so wet," he whispered in my ear. "Perhaps you speak the truth."

"Yes." I groaned, grinding my hips against his hand, letting my body become his as he sent his fingers into me. I was willing to do anything to please him. I dug my fingernails into his strong back, feeling the skin loosen slightly under my fingertips. The warm, wet stickiness of his blood covered them.

"Yes, that's it," he growled. "You want more?"

He slapped me hard on the thigh, growing more aroused.

I fell into the sheets of the bed, feeling a delicious tinge of electricity radiate down my leg.

Crouching above me like a tiger, he immediately reclaimed me. He pulled me from the bed, whirled me around, and wrapped his arms around me possessively. His fangs brushed the side of my shoulder.

Momentarily, I winced in shame when I realized my shoulders had dropped forward like a coward. I was shaking.

Suddenly, he grew very still. "I'll release you, if you like. And this will all be over. If I turn you, we'll surely go to war. Do you understand?" His breath was hot on my shoulder.

Gathering my strength, I locked myself into his embrace. My head fit perfectly in the hollow between his shoulder and neck. I settled back, enjoying the feel of his strong arms around me.

He traced his fingers down the outer curves of my body.

I could feel his heavy breathing on the back of my neck as he held me close. Then, putting a large hand to the front of my belly, he drew me to him.

"But I can't lose you," he whispered in my ear.

I shuddered beneath his touch. *To be his forever.*

"Do you want this?"

Silently, I took one of my fingers into my mouth while offering him the other hand. I licked away his blood, drawing the flavor in deeply. A taste of honey and salt radiated through my mouth. It was warm and inviting. He had to know I loved him.

He suckled my fingers and tasted his own blood.

Then, something intense flared in his movements as another low growl rumbled in his chest. He bent me over in front of him, lifting me slightly, and plunged his manhood fiercely, almost violently, into me.

"I don't want to leave you. I don't," I screamed as he pounded his hips against mine.

Throwing my head forwards, I pressed my body against his as I offered myself completely to his wonderfully, powerful thrusts. His male scent, a dark, rich fragrance of spice merged with my own like leather and silk, enveloping me and igniting my wet pussy.

As he hastened his pace, lengthening his stride deeper and deeper in me, an orgasm shuddered uncontrollably through my body. Two more followed.

He slowed his rhythm, but remained inside me. Sweeping me up into his strong arms, he turned me around so that I sat on his lower hips, straddling him. He lavished kisses along my breasts and neck. "I knew you were the one, Caroline."

I trembled, feeling the rush of passion race down my spine as I heard him say my name. He held me in his arms and I knew I was safe with him.

"Summon the Moon Goddess. She will guide you," he said.

I did as he commanded.

Suddenly, as clouds retreated into the northern sky, the moonlight flooded the room and illuminated him. He was devastatingly handsome with raven black hair framing his rugged face, high cheekbones, a perfectly straight nose, square jaw, and his drop-dead turquoise blue bedroom eyes that blazed with passion.

I felt his cock pulsate against my inner walls. They were swollen with lust and desire. I was still burning with passion for him as my juices dripped down the inside of my thighs.

The thought of my vampire lover biting me made me wild with yearning. A vampire biting another was an offering of blood love, he had said. It was very sacred, very precious, and not to be broken or taken lightly. We'd be bound together as husband and wife, for eternities. I didn't know if I could give myself to him like that, but I desperately wanted to. I wanted to come again and again and again for him like this forever, for eternities. Would my being a werewolf matter?

Seeing a glimpse of his fangs appear between his lush lips as he resumed his strides, holding me tenderly and kissing my cheek again, I moaned unable to stop an orgasm rising in me. I clung to him.

"Don't hold back this time. I will bite you when the Wolf comes for you. Just tell me when. You'll be okay. I'm here. Taste my blood again."

I felt his warm, wet tongue dart in my mouth, suckling my bottom lip. A sting of pain surfaced.

I shrieked, quickly pulling away from him.

He held me fast in his arms. Again, I tasted the sweetness of blood, but this time it was my own. Carefully, I licked my bottom lip where he had bitten me. Our eyes locked.

A surge of ecstasy rocked through me, similar to the feeling I had had when I first met him under our terrible beginning circumstances. I recognized it then, just as I recognized it now. He was the other part of my being, the other half of my heart. A very unlikely find in a non-werewolf creature outside my pack and outside my realm, but there he was. And I knew it as I met his gaze. His gaze devoured me. My vampire lover. My soul mate. *La mia ragione di vita.* My reason for living.

"You complete me," he said.

I traced the outline of his square jaw and rested the tip of my finger in his cleft of his chin. "*La mia ragione di vita,*" I replied in the language of Fanged that he had taught me over the past few months, meaning "my reason for living."

Another gleam from the moon shone upon his face, his bright eyes sparkled with a savage knowledge beyond lust and desire, one of sheer hunger. *He would be mine.*

Before I could stop him, he slashed at his well-toned chest with his nails. Lines of blood formed across his muscles.

"Drink of me."

Then he resumed making love to me fiercely, refusing to stop.

I stared at the streams of blood rolling down his chest as I rode him. With only a few thrusts from my vampire lover, the Wolf in me instantly awoke. Warm rushes of power and hunger rose up in me. The Wolf was coming for me and I wouldn't be able to deny him.

"Let it go," he whispered. "Drink of me."

The moon bathed him in its lush glow and I couldn't resist marveling at his naked form. He was exquisite. His thick, muscular chest glistened with blood and sweat and I held onto his shoulders as I drove my hips down upon him, feeling his magnificent cock surge deep inside me. Each stride I took sent me ever closer to him forever. I took his mouth with a savage intensity I had never known and then I lavished my kisses upon his chest, licking his blood and sweat in long, broad laps.

We will be together.

I leaned my head back, exposing my neck completely. "Do it. Do it now. He's here!"

Answering my request, he pulled me into his embrace and sank his teeth into my neck.

I cried out, instantly thrusting myself upwards to meet his fanged kiss. A flood of raw, electrifying sensations exploded inside me and multiple orgasms rocketed through my body.

He lifted me slightly off the bed and drank from me, holding me gently in his arms the whole time.

I pressed my back into his firm hands and focused on meeting his tempo as I rode him. The room began to spin. Blood trickled down my chest, running past my belly button and along the inside of my thighs. A delightful shiver of fear passed through me as my vampire lover shuddered and came inside me. *I will be his.*

REDEMPTION: MY VAMPIRE LOVER #2

(A Dark Realm Novella Series)

By

Victoria Embers

Author's Note: The second story, Redemption (My Vampire Lover #2) flashes back to when Caroline was first kidnapped by Raphael's father, Lord Asmoedus, and placed in Raphael's care. Excerpt consists of two chapters. Redemption will be available February 2013.

Chapter 1 - Raphael's Unexpected Delivery

Author's Note: This chapter is told from Raphael, the hero's point of view. Each chapter goes back and forth, sharing the hero and heroine's point of view.

Eight Months Earlier, in a Realm Far, Far away

"Who is that woman chained to my bed?"

Father didn't miss a beat when I stormed through the door of his study, unannounced. I thought he'd be shocked by my absurd question or at least annoyed by the intrusion of my six-foot, two-inch frame. He wasn't, and that worried me. He was up to something. Placing his journal on the huge mahogany desk, he then took his time to stuff the book and some papers in a drawer and lock it. As he tucked the key in the front pocket of his red silk vest, he buttoned his black velvet smoking jacket, retrieved his pipe, tapped it a few times on the desk, and then met my gaze, acting not the least bit surprised by the interruption.

"That woman is your new pet." He shook a long, bony red index finger at me and made his way around the desk to perch on one corner. For a few moments, he stared at the wall of bronzed werewolf skulls he had collected, waiting to see if I'd inquire about a few new additions. I didn't take the bait. I did notice, however, one was female, one male. He made no distinction between gender. A kill was a kill. If asked by a stranger how he gathered his collection of trophies, he'd boast he had received them all as tokens of appreciation for being such an honorable leader, which was a lie. Father had killed each and every one of them in his sick games, games I refused to participate in. I may be a warrior protecting the realm, but Father was a sadistic hunter, one who needed to be destroyed.

Finally, he returned his attention to me. His human eyes rolled over and changed to a blood red as his pupils dilated, disappeared, and formed menacing glowing orbs. He thought his monster face would scare me.

I didn't flinch. "I don't need a pet, Father."

"I handpicked her for you, my boy. I thought you'd be grateful." Snapping his fingers, a fire spark ignited at the tip end of his index finger and he used it to light his pipe. He inhaled deeply, taking a second or two to size me up until he finally released a puff of smoke in my direction.

"I won't play your games."

"Oh yes, you will," he snapped. "You're going to be on the field this year. That bitch is the cream of the crop. She'll perform well. I hear tell she's a Livonian werewolf. And guess whose daughter she is?"

I remained silent.

"You give up?" he asked. His eyes returned to their more humanistic qualities as he situated his vest.

Immediately not wanting to hear anymore, I crossed my arms and leaned slightly against the doorframe, refusing to answer or enter the room entirely. I also cocked my right foot in front of the left, letting the steel toe of my black leather boot smack firmly on the freshly polished wood floors. Surely that would leave a nice scratch for one of his staff members to buff out later.

He didn't seem to mind. His excitement took precedence over the condition of his precious treasures in his finely decorated office, or the floors for that matter. Father and his schemes. He and his brothers – my uncles, who I refused to claim any relation to other than we were all a part of the same underworld known as the Dark realm - acted like six-year-olds when it came to the Season of the Games or they figured out some cunning ploy to irritate the Golden realm, the latter plan which usually ended up being very stupid or one some person, mainly me, had to clean up. My patience thinning, I sighed and observed him.

My father was one of the seven lords of the Dark realm and he was a demon like all his brothers. He was called Asmodeus, a Latin word meaning "king of demons" that he preferred to be called because 1) he thought it meant he actually was king of the Dark realm, which he wasn't and 2) his brothers had put him in charge of recording all their adventures whether they were true or not. It was a task he prided himself on even though he had yet to print the first story. Scribbling down notes in between smoke breaks seemed to be his approach.

I was looking forward to the day when the real King of the Dark realm, Sarif, would ask my father where the book was. *That* would be fun.

Until then, playing the part instead of doing the work was my father's past time. He delighted in dressing up like a scholarly gentleman on his way to a speaking engagement in a dark three-piece suit with matching vest, top hat, tails and pointy leather shoes, despite his thick purplish red skin, two-inch frontal horns that he hid with his hat, and assortment of face piercings given to him every one hundred years, marking his birthday. With all his pomp and circumstance, my friend, Orlando and I had given him another name we used quite often when discussing his latest idiotic idea. It fit my father better and was much easier to say. Asshole.

"Ralph, my boy, I snagged old Lycaon's only daughter. It was so simple. In my disguise I dreamed up – not this of course – I was a Well, never mind. Anyways, she came right up to me. It was so easy. I fear she's not very bright, but that won't matter. I'm sure she'll do well in the games." In between puffs on his pipe, Father produced a series of wide grins that showed off a mouth full of yellowed fangs.

"My name is not Ralph," I uttered through clenched teeth.

"You know what I meant, Raphael." He pronounced my name with a grand amount of sarcasm and disgust.

"You kidnapped the Werewolf King's only daughter? The Princess of the Golden realm? And you want her in the games? Tell me you cleared this with one of your brothers?" I rarely indulged in listening to my father's ridiculous schemes, but this one was beyond insane if I had my facts right about who the woman was. Immediately, I cursed the fact that my father was not as well read as I was or he'd know his Lunar mythology. He won't be getting a kill this round, not if I could help it.

"Nope. Don't need 'em on this one. Our city is hosting the games this year. I have news for my brothers. We're going to win. And you, my boy, will lead that werewolf into the games."

"I have my dragon, Father. I don't need a werewolf."

"That dragon has seen better days. Besides, a werewolf will give you an edge, a sexy edge." He roared with laughter as a ring of smoke rose above his head.

"I realize Sarif is busy, but you at least notified Mammon about this. Didn't you?" I attempted to bring him back to reality with my subtle threat.

"No."

"Belphegor, then?"

"No." He threw his hands up in the air. "Honestly, where is your spirit of adventure? I have it in me because I write about it every day." He thumped his chest with pride. "I suppose you do not. You're a pale-face hybrid. Plain as vanilla. With no imagination. Why did I get such a useless son?"

"You don't have to make this personal, Father. I may be simply a vampire, but I'm also a warrior of the Dark realm. I serve to protect others and keep the peace. I don't need to look for adventure. You find enough 'adventure' for me to clean up as it is."

"You are such a dumb brute," he said. "You think being a warrior makes you important among us demons? You're a fly on my ass. That is all!"

Refusing to get into a shouting match with him because the door remained open, I held my tongue. Instead, I shut the door to his study and assumed a calm, yet defensive position. Hearing his lack of love for me always reminded me that my chosen path was the correct one. I didn't want to be the man he was. Not now. Not ever. I didn't want to rule the Dark realm in the condition it was currently in. Things needed to change.

His passive aggressive nature tempted me to lose my temper, but I wouldn't do it. *He* was the one who lacked imagination. Instead, I straightened my back and legs, crossed my arms, dug my nails into my well-toned biceps, and glared down at my father. Given his short stature of five feet, it was easy to do. It pleased him to remind me of my lineage. He may be my demon father, but my mother was human and I favored her ancestors, not his or that of his brothers. He delighted in reminding me of that.

I had the same bright blue eyes, pale complexion, and shiny raven black hair as my mother did. From her journals and letters I had obtained, I read that she dreamed about my growing up to overthrow my father someday and becoming a "great divine warrior," as she phrased it. One day, I would have revenge because my father was the reason I could no longer see my mother. He had banished her to the Beyond and I had yet to discover if she was alive or dead. There would be Hell to pay if she was dead. That I knew.

Father's voice brought me back to reality as my nerves gnawed a hole in my stomach. "I don't have to run every single idea by my brothers. All I have to do is create some havoc for the werewolves now and then. They'll love this plan. When opportunity comes knocking, what am I to do? Look away? I think not. And what better opportunity than kidnapping Lycaon's daughter? She's a peach, my boy. Not the brightest star in the cosmos, but she'll make a great pet."

"If she's a Livonian werewolf, Father, that means she's bound to the Moon Goddess and she's a threat to us. Do you really want the Moon Goddess showing up and blasting us to Kingdom Come or exiling us to the Land of Intolerables?" I asked.

Father scoffed at me, repeatedly rubbing the lapels of his velvet jacket with one hand as he chewed on the tip of his pipe with the other. I had hit a nerve. He and I both knew living in our city of Asmodian was fine, but being banished to the Land of Intolerables, a place inhabited with creatures far scarier than either of us. It was a thought neither of us wanted to entertain.

"No one has seen the Moon Goddess in centuries," he replied. "She doesn't exist. That's a myth Lycaon came up with to protect the Golden realm, and so is that Livonian werewolf crap. They can't keep us out and I proved that today. The Golden realm has no one protecting it. The Moon Goddess is gone. Wait until your uncles hear about this! They'll owe me!" He bounced around his desk like a school kid.

"You've taken leave of your senses. This will plunge us into war."

"Doubtful. I bet Lycaon won't even notice she's missing. She's a female, remember? They don't count unless they are dead." He laughed again. "Don't worry. I'll return her at some point or get rid of her. Yes, I'll get rid of her and add her to my wall, with the rest of her family." His eyes glowed and he glanced over at me. Quickly, he looked away when he saw I was not amused. "But don't you get any bright ideas. You're not letting her escape. I mean what I say. She's to be your pet and presented at the first tournament, or else."

I turned on my heel, not waiting to hear anything more my father had to say. Staying out of this shit storm had suddenly disappeared as an option.

~ ~ * ~ ~

"Sir, I did the best I could. I had to settle her down before she created an incident." One of my domestic assistants, Frederic met me at the door to my bedroom. His agitated demeanor was on overdrive. He raked his fingers through his wavy red hair as his eyes darted from side to side, avoiding making eye contact with me. Being a werecat, the presence of a wolf sent him over the edge.

"What did you do, Fredric?" I inquired, attempting to appear calm.

"I had to think of something quick. She broke her chains and was shifting all over the place. I had to protect myself and I couldn't let her escape, sir."

"That's fine. I'll see to it now, Fredric. Thank you."

"Yes, sir. I'm sorry I couldn't help more."

I nodded, hoping my loyal friend of many years, would adopt the same composure before someone from Father's staff heard us.

Fredric stood frozen in his tracks, his eyes remaining very wide as he rapidly blinked his eye lids and twitched his nose and lips. Werecats were skittish forest creatures.

"Bring me some refreshments, towels, soap, that sort of thing. Okay? Leave them by the door here."

"Yes, sir."

"Thank you, Fredric. That will be all."

"Oh, sir, should I get her some clothes or something?" Cautiously, he backed away from the door when he heard a thud on the other side.

I smiled at him, keeping my fangs hidden from view. In a normal situation, I thought, I would have said yes. But this was not going to be a normal situation. Far from it.

"She's a gift from my father, a pet. She's to serve me…" I paused for a moment, searching for the proper phrase of words.

"In the games, sir?"

"Yes, among other things," I mumbled. "Okay?"

Fredric's pale face turned beet red. "Yes, sir. Of course, sir. Thank you, sir. I'm sorry. Yes, okay. Thank you, sir. Thank you."

~ ~ * ~ ~

Knowing it wouldn't take Father long to find an excuse to stop by my chambers and check in on the woman, I quickly considered my options. As I watched Fredric scurry down the hallway, I entered through the door of my library, adjacent to the bedroom. I shut the door and glanced about the room. I waited and listened. The thudding sound had subsided. Assuming the woman was loose in my room, I decided it would be best to materialize instead of walking through the door and possibly frightening her again. I retrieved the bottle of potion Orlando had given me from a hidden compartment in one of the large walnut bookcases that surrounded my library and drank down the contents. Instantly, I vaporized into a trail of blue smoke and found my way through the locked bedroom keyhole.

Nothing could have prepared me for the scene in my bedroom. The startling realization of seeing the woman in wolf form crammed into a wire cage jolted me out of my vapor form. I fell to the floor in a heap. I'd have to speak to Fredric immediately. She wasn't going to remain in a cage.

I approached her.

She growled, showing me her sparkling white fangs and her thick, light beige fur rising along the ridge of her back. She slammed into cage a few times, threatening to attack if she could break free. Once she stopped moving, she continued to watch me with angry eyes, her head swaying back and forth like a snowy owl, all the time remaining defiant, fearless, and ready to kill me at a moment's notice.

I knelt before her, hoping my research on Lunar mythology was accurate. A wolf chant may calm her down. I had to reason with her in this form before Father arrived. But would she understand me? Would the chant work?

I spoke to her in the language my mother had taught me. It was the language of the Fanged world and allowed me to speak with many others who practiced the Magics. Maybe I could convince her I wasn't a threat. "*Una bellezza come nessun altro. Così bella. Calmati. Calmati. Io non ho intenzione di permettere a nessuno di farti del male.*"

Her eyes glowed a magnificent shade of amber, unlike anything I had ever seen before.

I repeated the phrase again and again and again. It didn't matter what I said as long as I repeated it, like a chant. Quickly, I sped through the words. I wanted her to know she was safe.

Her eyes flashed and she slumped down, touching the steel surface of the cage and slightly whining as she placed her paws over her head. *Damn it. I spoke too rapidly. She was in pain.*

"Come on, Raphael. You can do this. It's a lot like snake charming." I laughed at that last statement I said to myself, recalling the last time I had seen my uncle Sarif in snake form. A giant black cobra, arching ten feet in the sky, spitting fire down on his servants like a crazed dragon when they failed to prepare enough meat for the feast. That had been a fun family visit.

I returned my attention to the she-wolf. I said the chant again, this time slowly, softly, and with feeling.

After a few moments, her back legs slouched and collapsed on the bottom of the cage. She continued to glare at me. I held her gaze, commanding her to hear me. *I'll help you get out of here, but you've got to trust me.* Soon enough, her eyelids grew heavy and she passed out. *Welcome to Hell, little one,* I mentally added, knowing the connection was broken.

"Raphael, how are we doing in there?"

Father's voice boomed from my library, instantly bringing me to my senses.

~ ~ * ~ ~

I slammed the bedroom door behind me, forgetting the noise would likely disturb my guest. "It's a mess in there, Father. I can't let you in."

"I'm not interested in your interior decorating or lack of. It's not like you have any," he said, probably referring to my simple attire of a black fitted T-shirt and black leather pants to go with my steel-toed leather boots or my few pieces of furniture in my rooms. I spent my earnings on weapons or books, not meaningless knick-knacks like he did.

"I have things under control here," I announced.

"I'd like to visit our pretty pet."

"She's not 'our pet.' She's mine, remember? Besides, she needs time to adjust. She's not exactly happy with this situation." I continued to block the door as he wandered around my library.

He noticed the small bottle of potion on the floor and sauntered over to where it was. He picked it up and examined it carefully as he spoke. "She's still in wolf form, then?"

"I'm afraid so. We wrestled and I knocked her out," I lied. In my haste, I had made a grave error.

"Pity. I was hoping to get a look at her this evening before the hunt. I hate hunting on the grounds, but perhaps the tents by the stadium are set up already. I may go over there. Care to join me?" He strolled around my desk in his hunting outfit, a long red riding coat over a silk shirt with white slacks stuffed into black leather riding boots. He tossed the bottle near a stack of books.

"I have my blood tea. Thank you just the same."

He arched his eyebrow at me, clearly displeased with my answer. He was extremely hungry and it showed. I wasn't letting him anywhere near the she-wolf. His wrinkled face and sunken eyes reminded me of the welcoming globes that would be used to light the roads leading to the stadium for the games.

"Perhaps another time."

"Certainly," I replied as I impatiently waited for him to make his way across the room and out the door.

"My boy?"

"Yes, Father?"

"Just because your mother was a sorceress doesn't mean I want you dabbling in Black Magic. You were born a vampire and you'll remain as such. I'll not have you become a threat too, so no hocus pocus."

Before he could finish his second threat for the day, I added "or else" and nodded with an over-exaggerated bow of sarcastic respect. "I may be a warrior, protecting the Dark realm, but I know my place in your city. I'd never jeopardize my standing among the guard," I announced.

"Just so we are clear."

"Crystal," I snapped, not caring if that implied I'd be consulting my crystal ball later. I didn't own one. The realization that he referred to my mother in past tense startled me. *She couldn't be dead. You, cocksucker, if you killed her...*

I turned around to return to the bedroom when I heard the library door open again. I hissed and dropped my fangs in that direction, ready for the threat. Father stood, holding the door ajar for two of his staff members as they slunk into the room. One deposited the bathing supplies on my leather couch while the other dumped several feet of chain and a black dog collar on the Persian rug in the center of my library.

Both held their heads low until Father summoned them with a cluck of his tongue. He followed the domesticated hellhounds to the door.

"By the way, genius, silver paralyzes the movements of werewolves. Unlike the others, *these* chains should keep your pet in her place. I *will* see her the next time I visit."

Mentally, I heard the threat with his "or else" words again being added, despite the fact I had not heard him utter them. My father, Lord Asmodeus, was spectacular at being an asshole. I had to come up with a plan and fast.

Chapter 2 - Caroline's Realization

The minute I awoke, I knew I was alone. For how long I had been alone, I didn't know. "*Move, Caroline. Move,*" I thought to myself. Cold steel stung my naked flesh and I realized I was finally in my human form. I opened the door to the cage and wiggled my way out.

The bedroom was sparsely decorated with only a few items positioned strategically in the room. The enormity of it halted me in my tracks as I searched for something to put on. A square dining table that doubled as a writing desk and nightstand was shoved up against the wall next to the largest Victorian four poster bed I had ever seen. A pile of books and papers were scattered on the table amid a few small blue glass bottles, bowls, and ceramic cups. Almost touching the seven-foot-tall wooden ceiling, the bed was made of the same red mahogany wood and had a green velvet bedspread and curtains lined with gold tassels. The bed stood on a plush forest green and tan rug that peeked a few feet out from beneath the bed. Clearly, a man had decorated this room, but what kind of man? A giant?

"I hate hunting on the grounds this close to the games. Will you join me, perhaps?"

When I heard voices in the other room, I dove into the closet. *Weapons,* I thought. *Clothes or weapons. What can I use as a weapon?* I stood frozen in fear, contemplating, questioning my every move. *How was I going to do this?* My hands began to tremble uncontrollably. *Control, Caroline. Get control of yourself.*

Immediately, I called upon my wolf sense, the wonderfully intuitive side of my lunar nature that kept me balanced, focused, and ready to take on the world. A warmness settled in my stomach and I stretched my neck through a man's long-sleeved shirt that reminded me of silk. Problem One solved. I realized I'd be sore for weeks after shifting half a dozen times because of my human fright, but I pushed that to the back of my mind. I continued to search through the closet, and then suddenly felt cold steel. *These will do.*

Exiting the closet, I raised my nose in the air and breathed in, hoping to understand my surrounds. *Wolf, where are we?*

In the land of demons.

~ ~ * ~ ~

When the door partially opened, I took aim at a large, dark figure and threw the first knife of several I had found in the closet at the person as he came into view. I stood behind the massive bed, using it as a bunker. This demon was not going to take me alive.

The figure grunted, slumping slightly to the ground.

I heard the weapon I had thrown at him fall to the floor.

My aim was bad and had not found the demon's heart. I was at a great disadvantage. "You stay back, demon!" I shouted, hoping to sound far more threatening than I'm sure I appeared to be. "I've got more where that came from!" Dripping wet, I was maybe one hundred pounds. Cold, weak from hunger, and nearly naked, I was half of that, I was sure. Or at least I felt like that. Adrenaline and self-preservation would have to see me through, so I could complete my mission.

"Do your worst," the tall figure announced. "However, I'd like to ask if I may turn on a few lights before you continue your attack. If you don't mind?"

He mocked me, which should have infuriated me even more, but I held my position and watched as he illuminated the room. He flipped a few switches by the doorframe and the room took on a blue hue like it had been bathed in the soft, gentle lights from beneath the sea.

I looked up at the ceiling just as the wooden beams filed away to two corners. "How did you do that?" I gasped, forgetting my defensive stance all together.

"I can't handle fluorescent lighting, so I had these installed. Blue is my favorite color, actually, even though I wear a lot of black. Here, let me show you one more thing. I just had this done."

He raised his muscular arm upwards and pressed a button at the top of the doorframe.

I blinked my eyes several times, getting used to the various colors I saw forming on the ceiling. An image was being constructed.

The lighted design was magnificent and took my breath away. A variety of shades of blue, green, and purple illuminated behind the picture of a warrior riding a fierce dragon. The dragon stood on a set of rocks jutting out from the edge of a cliff with its head held high and proud. The warrior wore silver armor, waving a lance in one hand as he looked across the horizon while perched on his dragon. *A strong image of a strong warrior and his companion preparing for battle. Why would a demon have such an image promoting the bond of man and creature fashioned on the ceiling of his bedroom? It didn't make sense.*

"I've never seen anything like it. Is that you?"

"More or less. My friend, Orlando, created it and installed it for me. I'm not really an admirer of art or paintings. I'm more interested in books, mythology really, but Orlando thought this would dress up my bedroom. I mainly like it for the quiet motivation it gives me. Each day is a test, a determining factor of what kind of man I am going to be that day. It helps me remember, despite everything, who I really am."

"What kind of demon are you?" I blurted out.

Instantly, he crossed the room towards me. He had his large hands wrapped around my elbows before I could grab another knife. I was pinned against his brawny chest. The minute our eyes met, a bolt of lightning felt like it had ricocheted through my body. My eyes widened as he let me go and I wrapped my arms tightly around my body, so I wouldn't fall. He staggered for a moment too, like he'd been hit by a burst of energy.

The immediate recognition of a soul mate was something that did not occur outside the pack. It had to be a mistake. But was it? It felt so real. In that second, I re-evaluated my course of action.

"I'm not a demon. I'm a vampire," he replied as he put some distance between us. "There's a difference." He retreated to the table and sat down. He remained quiet for some time, and then said, "If you must know, I prefer to be called a warrior above all else."

I thought about asking a second question like 'Why did you kidnap me?' but I remained silent. It didn't really matter as long as I found my target. The accusation of calling him a demon seemed to have gravely offended him and I instinctually wanted to comfort him. *Why would I want to do that? He was the enemy.* I opted to use my charms on the man. *Violence would get me nowhere with him.*

"I like the ceiling painting," I said instead.

"Thank you. It's very nice, isn't it?"

"Do you have a name, vaaa ...?" I abruptly stopped before I insulted him again.

"Raphael."

I waited for him to ask my name. He studied the table instead.

"I'm Caroline," I offered.

"Caroline." He repeated my name slowly and carefully as if it was a foreign word he didn't want to forget.

"Your name is very unique." A few compliments couldn't hurt. "What does Raphael mean?"

"I've never thought to look it up. I don't know."

I watched as he drew a few curves and lines along the table, absent-mindedly tracing something. "If my memory serves me right, I think Raphael means healer."

He grunted.

Knowing I'd probably upset him again if I said it too loud, I mumbled under my breath as I attempted to process the realization. "A healing vampire? Isn't that an oxymoron?"

"Perhaps it is," he answered. "You forget. I have excellent hearing too. What does your name mean?"

The second knife flew from my hands and slammed into the wooden table, a few inches from his hands.

He didn't flinch one inch.

"Freedom," I announced as I swiftly bent over to retrieve another knife lying on the bed.

"Well that's good. Freedom for Caroline. I like that." There was a trace of laughter in his voice. He paused for a moment before he continued. "I know this is highly unorthodox and you're in an extremely frightening situation. I want to put your mind at ease, however. I'm not interested in harming you. I know you are of great importance to your people. I'm going to try to get you out of here, but you're going to have to trust me. It's as simple as that. Do you think you can do that?" He yanked the knife from the table and, with an ironically tender touch, he bent the blade into a slight arch, disabling it so it couldn't be used for anything but holding a bottle of wine or large orange. I swallowed hard, so my mouth wouldn't drop open. *This vampire could kill me in an instant.*

Suddenly, a vision from my wolf state hit me. I recognized his voice. *I'll help you get out of here, but you've got to trust me.* I closed my eyes and relived the moment again. *"Una bellezza come nessun altro. Così bella. Calmati. Calmati. Io non ho intenzione di permettere a nessuno di farti del male."* Over and over again, that voice. A ripple of awareness surged through me. His voice was the same as the man who had come to me to console me in my agitated wolf state. It was deep, almost sensual, yet tranquil and protective. It was this man before me who had calmed me. "The wolf chant. That was *you*?"

"Yes."

"What did you say?"

He paused for a moment, digging his long nail into the wood of the table. "That's not really important, is it?"

"I insist," I replied with my polite royal tone I used when I wanted it to be known I expected to get what I sought.

He chuckled. His laugh was low and throaty. "I've seen pomp and circumstance from my father. You don't have to take that tone with me. There is no need for hierarchy."

I attempted to soften my insistence. "I'm sorry. Please, then."

"Don't apologize. Let's keep this a level playing field. I treat you as an equal and you treat me as one. Okay?"

His confidence was infectious.

"Fair enough," I whispered, only realizing a second later that I had not fully enunciated the words. *This man clearly had not kidnapped me so why was I in his presence? Did he know who had kidnapped me? Maybe he could lead me to the person? Equals? Why would he say we were equals? Men in my realm certainly didn't think like that. His words and actions of kindness and hospitality thoroughly confused me.* As a sign of good faith, I placed the weapons down before me on the bed, noticing in passing the letter "R" carved into the blade of each knife. *I needed to know more before I made my move.*

"A beauty like no other. So beautiful. Calm yourself. Calm yourself, my sweet. I'm not going to let anyone hurt you."

"I'm sorry? What did you say?"

He repeated his words for my benefit.

I replied, "No demon would know how to practice Wolfen Magic." I observed his new nervousness. His mood had shifted and he refused to look at me as he continued to scratch at the table.

"I'm not a demon. I'm a vampire. I'm a warrior, a vampire warrior." He glanced at the ceiling, looking again at the lighted design of the warrior and dragon. "I thought we covered that?" His tone was very gentle, even though I saw the muscles in his jaw twitch a few times.

"Raphael, the vampire warrior, it's a pleasure to meet you." I curtsied, trying to appear more of a princess than I felt as well as lighten the mood.

The intensity of his serious face vanished and he laughed as he stood up from the table. Watching his contentment was like observing Zeus shower the Earth with the Northern Lights when he was in a good disposition. It immediately put me at ease as well.

"My mother is a sorceress, so yes, I dabble in the Magics. And I bet I know more about Wolfen Magic than you do," he bragged.

"That's probably true. I know nothing about magic. Only the Wolf guides me."

257

"Perhaps I can teach you some." His smile was radiant, confident, and proud. His demeanor changed frequently. *Was there such a thing as a moody vampire*, I wondered.

When he turned and looked directly at me, my heart splintered into a million pieces as I witnessed the expression on his face. *Wolf, what has befallen upon me?* Despite my confusion, I returned a half-heartedly crooked smile in his direction from across the room as my mouth fell open slightly, instantly forgetting why I was there. I was speechless to do otherwise. This man, this vampire, was a vision of sheer beauty and he wanted to help me. Moreover, he instantly trusted me. A person he didn't know. He trusted me. *A warrior who understands and strives to be honest, loyal, and trustworthy. A man like no other. A vampire. Maybe. A demon? Never!*

Within seconds, his dark, broody stare had transformed to a delightful, glorious appearance. That essence of love came from his heart. From what my aunt had told me, no demon could fake love or real concern for another. They didn't possess it. This man. Raphael, as he was called, was a real warrior. A vampire, a man, and a warrior. All in one. No trace of a demon at all. I couldn't form a simple word to respond. The attraction I felt pooling up in the pit of my stomach was undeniable. *But how could this be? And more importantly, why? Why would I feel an instant attraction to a different species?* I instantly realized I couldn't kill him. I couldn't think straight. Actually, I couldn't think at all. I simply returned his gaze, letting myself be taken in by his eyes.

Our silence intensified as I studied him. He returned my gaze without shame, looking into my very soul it seemed.

Raphael was tall with a well-toned physique, and long muscular arms and legs. He defined every square inch of his clothing perfectly – like a warrior – as he stood there watching me in his black fitted T-shirt, tight leather pants, and bulky leather boots. But none of that should have registered with me as I continued to watch him, but it did. His facial expression said it all. It was a familiar fondness like he had known me all his life, unashamed and comforting, as if I were a lover who had discovered her way back to him. Despite my duty, I wanted to run and jump in his arms, smothering his handsome, rugged face with kisses. He sealed my fate with his eyes. No man had ever looked at me with such desire. It overwhelmed and I knew my life would never be the same from that day forward.

Before I realized it, he crossed the room. In my disoriented mood, I let him pick me up and sit me on his bed in front of him. To my astonishment, he knelt before me, brushing away the remaining knives to the center of the bed behind me. He let his hands linger on my naked knees and immediately rushes of warmth radiated in every direction along my upper thighs and lower legs. His shirt, the one I wore, was the only thing that divided us. I swallowed hard, trying to dispose of my immediate attraction for him. *Wolf, what has certainly befallen me?*

The curse of true love.

"I know we just met and this is the worst way to meet someone..." The rich timbre of Raphael's voice surprised me. "But you seem like a nice, pleasant person and I wouldn't want anything to happen to you. Caroline, I'll get you out of here. That I can promise you, but this is a strange and dangerous place. And at all times, I want you to promise; you will stay by my side. No matter what you see or hear. Do you understand?"

I nodded, swallowing again as I attempted to not roll my eyes at the polite command in his instructions. "I've been around," I challenged.

"Where am I exactly?" I asked, knowing already what the answer may be.

"I doubt you have been to a place like this. You are in the Dark realm, in the city of Asmodian. Lord Asmodeus is the ruler here. He kidnapped you and he'll put you in the games where you will be hunted and killed, preferably by him or one of his brothers. He has a wall of trophies in his study, featuring many of your species."

"What?" I screamed. My younger brother. My aunt. My blood instantly went cold.

"Shhh. Someone will hear you." He clamped his hand over my mouth and we fell onto the bed in each other's arms. He shifted his weight and I ended up on top of him. I could see the knives out of the corner of my vision. *It wouldn't be difficult to kill him from this vantage point. Did silver affect vampires the way it did werewolves?*

"If you want to use those knives, I suggest you go for my heart. But it won't do any good. In a place like this, I lost my heart long ago. You can't kill me. I was born as a vampire, a pureblood. I can't die."

How far could I get if I tried to kill this vampire? Was a vampire the same as a demon? I had heard only the vampires born were beyond death? Was that what he was? I couldn't stand the thought of killing him, even if it didn't work. My heart and soul raged at me. *Maybe he could be an ally instead.*

"Do you promise to help me escape?" I asked the question with as much innocence I could muster for a princess, a princess of a Werewolf King surely going mad. My world was turning into one of kill or be killed. *Should I kill this vampire and be done with it? Could I kill him despite his proclamations against the latter?*

His hands continued to rest on my now exposed thighs. I felt his fingertips delicately massaging the curve of my buttocks. It sent shivers of delight up my spine.

"I will help you, Caroline," he whispered. "I must."

"What will they do to us if we are caught?"

"Don't worry about me. I can handle it, but you. I'd rather not think about what they'd do to you before they kill you." His voice drifted off and his brilliant blue eyes glazed over. He turned his attention to my disarrayed shirt of his that I was wearing and gently smoothed it back into place. I marveled at how warm his touch was, how satisfying and soothing. The Wolf flashed a startlingly realization into my mind's eye. *Despite his inward struggles, it was obvious that this man's allegiance was to a greater good, not the evil permeating in the Dark realm. It was clear to see that he was above that. Raphael was a good man, a vampire warrior I had only read about in my aunt's books, the existence of which was rarely heard of anymore.*

As Raphael's hands paused on my shoulders, I asked, "Could you help me find some clothes I can travel in, please?"

"Of course. I apologize. You can't travel in just this shirt, now can you? I have to say blue suits you well." He chuckled and, whisking me off the bed, he headed for the closet, never once letting go of my hand. "Do as I say. Follow my lead and you'll be home before you know it. Agreed, Caroline?"

"Agreed." Hearing his congenial, yet authoritative tone, I gritted my teeth.

~ ~ * ~ ~

Raphael led me through a secret door in the closet of his bedroom I was surprised I had not found. We followed a long staircase down along a cave made of red stone that was hot to the touch. I felt clumsy and awkward wearing his oversized clothes, which consisted of a dark green jacket, a black long-sleeve shirt I tied into a knot at my waist, matching jeans and boots, and a knit cap he requested I stuff my hair under. As the delight of smelling his masculine scent on the articles of clothing washed over me, I tried my best to focus on the steps and stay close behind him, so I wouldn't fall against the wall. Once the staircase ended, we stood before a four-foot steel door that didn't seem to have a doorknob.

"How are we going to get through that?" I asked, motioning to him that both of us were taller than four feet.

For some reason, he found my question amusing. "Like this," he replied.

Suddenly he vanished before my eyes. All I could see was an immense cloud of blue smoke. Then I heard Raphael's voice. "I'll open the door from the other side."

When the door flew open, he stood there, fully clothed in his long leather trench coat, T-shirt, jeans, and boots like nothing had happened.

"Now that's some trick."

"I've got a few up my sleeves." He locked the door, checking the hinges and making sure all the corners of it remained secure. I admired his magnificent stature in the dim light. As I glanced around to see where the light source was coming from, I realized it was a red moon that peeked out occasionally from behind dark clouds.

"I've never seen a red moon," I commented, not really expecting a reply.

"I wouldn't expect so. We're near the center of the Earth." He paused for a moment and studied me. "Have you been to the center of the Earth?"

"No," I replied, hoping I sounded convincing.

He continued on. "Have your eyes adjusted yet?"

"Almost. Why?" I asked.

He nodded. "We have a long distance to cover quickly. I want to make sure you can keep up."

"I can keep up, fanger." My mother's blind arrogance immediately flared up in me, a trait I instantly regretted showing off.

His pleasant disposition turned dark. Momentarily, I took a step backwards, waiting to see what he'd do next. Being low on energy, I'd be unable to summon the Wolf in a moment's notice if he attacked me.

"Let's get something straight, Caroline," he said.

"I meant no offense," I offered gently, hoping to derail a fight. *I needed this man on my side.*

He sighed loudly and gathered my hands up in his. The warmth of his touch startled me and

I felt that spark again. *Weren't vampires supposed to be ice cold to the touch?* I studied his hands enveloping mine for a moment. In the low light, I couldn't see the details of his wonderful large hands, but I felt the strength, the raw energy charging through them. I was helpless to move as he towered over me and held me in his clutches. For a fleeting moment, fear surfaced in the back of my throat. I wanted to scream, yank my hands away, even if I didn't flee with both of them. I wanted to tell this vampire I needed no one's help, especially his. I was on a mission. I had to avenge my brother's death. And yet, I couldn't move. His presence overwhelmed me. His touch soothed me. His brooding stare mesmerized me. He was the essence of the Legend of Vampyre I had read about, the stories my aunt had shared with me as a child. She favored all supernatural creatures who fought for the well being of others, not the demons who only understood pain, torture, and death. Unfortunately, I had no understanding of that, while my younger brother had learned firsthand what the demons would do, but this vampire was different. In the short time I had known him, I already understood that. Aunt Elizabeth's words filtered through my mind. *"We have a lot to learn from them as well, Caroline."*

"I know we don't have much time, so I'd like to ask for your respect. I need your help actually. If you want to get out of here, I would expect you'd want to help me, right?"

"I was rude. I shouldn't have…" Raphael cut me off, continuing his dialogue.

"Yes, I'm a fanger, but there is a difference between me and the demons here. The people who will set you free are fangers too. They fight for good, not evil. I fight for good. You must understand that now. Just because you're a princess of the Golden realm doesn't mean you are the only one fighting for good. We're here, in the trenches every day, fighting for our salvation and yours, for the humanity of our worlds. If the Dark realm ever infests the Golden realm and extinguishes the Light, it'll be all over. Surely you can understand that, Caroline?"

Hearing his declarations of justice astounded me. I had found an ally and I understood his concerns only too well. He didn't know it, but we were on the same side. *He's one of us,* I told the Wolf. My heart exploded a second time. Each time he addressed me by my name, it collapsed my very soul. This vampire who I had known for as many hours as I could count on one hand spoke to me as an equal. Me, the kidnapped princess. Me, the assassin seeking revenge. I wasn't as innocent as I wanted Raphael to believe. And he wasn't as haughty as I wanted to presume him to be. I was a princess of a realm that held few joys for me since losing my brother and aunt. A realm that was in trouble because of my father's grief. His heart was growing darker by the day, and I knew I had to stop him. It was true, what my aunt had said to me the last days of her life. He'd follow my mother to a very dark place if someone did not stop them. And that would mean war. My world wasn't so different from this vampire's. Perhaps the Moon Goddess did have a plan for me after all, as my aunt had said.

Deciding to make a bold statement and seek his affection, I pushed my body into his. At first, our clasped hands rested just above my breasts, but I found my way into the side of his neck, letting my head rest there. Raphael was several inches taller than I was, at my stature of five feet, seven inches. Then, just as quickly as he had gathered my hands in his earlier, he wrapped his arms about mine. His moves were faster than my vision could understand. I relied on feeling his touch instead. *His embrace felt too right to be wrong*, I told myself.

When he finally spoke, Raphael's voice was only a whisper, but crisp and clear. "If I can do this, if I can get you out of here, I'll have saved at least one person. I couldn't save the others, but maybe you, Caroline; you will be my redemption."

My entire body went rigid in his arms. "What do you mean?"

"This is part of the demons' game. It's the hunt that entices them. When Asmodeus brings an unsuspecting person here, he sets a new path for them. If they fail, they die. We have to get to the river before they find us."

"How do you know he's after us?" I asked as I looked into his dark eyes, wanting to meet this Asmodeus and introduce him to the Wolf straight away.

"Trust me. I know. In his mind, the Season of the Games has already begun. And if he has realized you aren't in my rooms, which I suspect he has…" His voice trailed off as he looked out across the dark horizon. A great struggle raged in his soul. For a long time, he remained silent.

Then, finally, he embraced me again. "Not this time. He won't succeed this time."

The moment I felt his hand on the back of my neck, I moaned quietly. The emotions in me rose to the surface. I couldn't control it. And I couldn't deny it. I had found love in the most unlikely place, at the most unlikely time. I remained frozen in this vampire's grasp. If my freedom was at the hands of this vampire, so be it. If it meant losing my heart to him in the process, so be it. I wanted to spend eternities being in this man's arms. Forever. My mission? It could go to Hell.

Caroline, think with your head, not your slit. This vampire is the enemy too. We must destroy them all.

For the first time in my life, I ignored the Wolf.

"I'm sorry about before. I didn't realize my words would hurt you, Raphael. Please forgive me." I swallowed down the Wolf's words as I recognized the fact that my priorities were quickly changing.

You must avenge your loved one's death.

Raphael's arms tightened closer around me.

"If you can help me escape, I'll be in your debt," I stated as I returned his embrace, resuming my part.

Pulling away from me as he gazed into my eyes, he tucked a portion of my long blonde bangs under my cap again. He searched my face for answers. A million problems seemed to be knotted up behind his eyes. His brows drew together in an agonized expression. "You don't owe me anything. This is between me and Asmodeus – not you. These games must end now. I know that now. He'll never stop unless someone steps in."

His discourse didn't seem directed at me.

"I can say that I only wish we had met under more favorable circumstances because I fear that when you leave, you will be taking my heart with you."

Tears rose in my eyes and I pressed my face into his chest. "I'll keep it safe, Raphael. I promise. But first, I must tell you something." After realizing he had just handed his heart over to me, I decided to come clean and tell him everything. *Would he understand?*

Would the Wolf remain quiet if I shared the truth with Raphael?

To be continued...

About the Author

Victoria Embers is a stay-at-home mom who believes good romance should make you purr while good erotic romance should make you scream, but in a good way, of course. She loves embracing her obsession for vampires and werewolves and the naughty situations they find themselves in by writing steamy hot romances with a blend of paranormal romance, fantasy, and erotica.

Fanged to English Translations

The following are English translations for any words spoken in the language of the Fanged world, which is very similar to modern day Italian. Each is organized by chapter.

Prologue – Caroline's Awakening

La mia ragione di vita. = My reason for living.

Chapter 1 – Raphael's Unexpected Delivery

Una bellezza come nessun altro. Così bella. Calmati. Calmatevi, mio dolce. Io non ho intenzione di permettere a nessuno di farti del male. = A beauty like no other. So beautiful.

Calm yourself. Calm yourself, my sweet. I'm not going to let anyone hurt you.

AWAKENINGS: THE WRATH SAGA

An Excerpt

By

Will Van Stone Jr. & S.I. Hayes

Deep within the confines of Lafayette Cemetery No.2, Erik sat in perfect silence before an old crypt. The stone structure was awash in the dim yellow light of a flickering candle flame, which threw the dancing shadows of a single rose against the sealed entrance. Though just shy of one hundred years old, not a single imperfection could be found in its walls.

Erik extinguished the flame, put the candle back into the box he left by the crypt, and stood with his head bowed. He leaned in close to the engraving underneath the family crest and slid his finger along the chiseled letters as he whispered words under his breath. "Oh, Helena…" He closed his eyes, resting his head against the cold stone.

"She would want you to be a bit less… Loser."

"Go away, assassin." Erik hissed, refusing to look up.

"Is that any way to treat your ol' friend Diabolique?"

"Mist off, will you? I want to be alone."

Diabolique placed a hand on Erik's tense shoulder as she leaned in close to his ear. "I know it's been a while since a woman would touch you, but being pathetic isn't the way into her panties." Her tone was less than kind.

"Why are you still here?"

"While we've never really... Tolerated each other, I can't stand to see a full-grown... Man... Act like such a pussy."

"Go away."

"Fine... I have more interesting people to talk to tonight."

"Bitch..." Erik whispered when he realized she was gone. "Why Lyndsay insists on affiliating with such-"

"Where're you hiding?"

Erik's eyes flew open at the sound of Christopher's voice. He looked around quickly, spotting him a few rows over. He straightened up and slipped in between two crypts, sneaking up behind him.

"I thought you were hungry?" Erik asked.

Christopher spun around, surprised. "When did you get so sneaky?"

"Been watchin' you," Erik said, laughing as he jumped on top of the nearest crypt. He leaned back and crossed his ankles. "So, you have any fun?"

"Well," Christopher began, already sitting on the cracked stone slab. "While you were doing... Whatever it is you do when you're alone, *I* was meeting a rather intriguing young lady."

"Do tell." Erik smiled curiously.

"A gentleman never kisses and tells."

"And when I finally meet one, I'll remember that. C'mon, spill!" Erik pleaded, hands folded.

"Fine. Her name was Anne something or other. I met her on Chestnut and... She had long blond hair and even longer legs. And those lips I could tease for days... Then, when she told me she wasn't wearing anything underneath that barely there skirt, I decided to escort her home." Christopher smiled as he looked past Erik to a couple of girls who had just entered the cemetery.

"And... What happened next?"

"Why tell you when I can show you? Follow me. You can have the white girl."

Christopher hopped down and, with Erik just behind him, quietly came up behind the two scantily clad coeds, one fair and the other, to Christopher, the most beautiful shade of mocha. He could smell the alcohol and ecstasy running through them as they stumbled along the narrow paths between the burial markers.

"Jesus, Christie, are you sure we should be here?" the fair girl asked, clutching Christie's arm so tightly that the girl's fingers marked her satin skin.

"Calm down, Carolanne. We're just gonna have some fun," Christie said, pulling away from her friend's vise-like grip. "Got the candles?"

"Yea, in my bag-" Carolanne grabbed her shoulder and stopped. "Shit! Where'd it go?"

"What now?" Christie spun around and opened her mouth to yell seconds before it dropped.

"Christie?"

"Behind you…"

Carolanne spun around before falling back.

"Good evening, ladies. Are you sure you should be out alone so late at night?"

"Umm…" Carolanne managed.

"Don't worry. We thought you'd like a little company." Christopher handed Carolanne the bag. "I think you dropped this."

"Thank you…" She cleared her throat nervously.

"My name is Christopher and my shy little friend here is Erik. Might we join you? It can be dangerous here at night. You never know what nasty creatures may be lurking around every corner."

"When you put it that way," Christie said, wrapping her arms around his neck. "Maybe we could use some strong, sexy boys."

"Use me all you like."

"Christie…" the friend pleaded, unsure.

"Relax, Carolanne. What could possibly happen?" She pulled herself up and kissed Christopher as she dragged a leg up his thigh.

Christopher licked her neck and smiled. "Only good things…"

"What about me?" Carolanne whined, still on the ground.

"Don't worry my dear, my friend finds you rather... appetizing."

~ ~ * ~ ~

Christopher pinned Christie against an old rundown crypt and kissed her fast and hard as his hand traveled down her waist to what could barely be considered a skirt. She pushed his hand underneath the dark fabric and slid the tips of his fingers along the wetness of her skin before sliding them inside of her.

A gasp escaped from deep within her as a baser instinct took hold. She tore open her shirt and pressed her bare ebony beasts against him.

"Don't make me wait... Take me now!"

"Not just yet," he whispered. "Let's take our time." He looked over at Erik and smiled. "I want to savor you."

~ ~ * ~ ~

Erik stood stunned for a moment, strangely excited by Christopher's erotic display. *Girls have gotten so peculiar*, he mused silently as Carolanne dropped to her knees before him, unzipped his fly, and reached into his pants.

She searched for a moment, then pulled at him with a smile. "My, you do enjoy a good show." She opened her mouth and took him between her soft red lips.

His body tensed as her tongue bathed his hard flesh, sending convulsions racing through his nerves. His head jerked back as that tongue reached out to tease his tightening sac.

Giving into his body's urges, he pinned her against the crypt, undoing his pants further as he grabbed her hair and pounded into her mouth faster and harder with each thrust as her throat constricted in gags. He could feel the years of pent up frustration exploding out of him as he released down her throat.

He pulled away, feeling a bit ashamed. As he bent down to pull up his pants, she stopped him and threw him to the ground.

"Don't go yet. I wanna see what else that cock of yours can do."

~ ~ * ~ ~

Christopher pulled from the girl and wiped away the blood still on his lips. Lying there, in Death's sweet embrace, she looked like an angel; they always looked liked angels to him, though he knew her blood too well now to believe lies such as that. *What a waste... I forgive you.* He made a subtle gesture of the cross before looking behind him, finding Carolanne riding Erik hard, as though she knew would never know a man that way again. With a dry smile, he made his way to them and stood quietly watching until they finally noticed him.

"What happened to Christie?"

"Oh, she's regrouping." He smirked, pushing his hair from his face.

"That's too bad." Her eyes met his before they slid down the length of his body. "And look, she didn't even let you finish. It's a pity to waste a… gift… like that." She turned back to Erik, who writhed under her body with each movement she made. "Can your friend join us?"

"Yea, E," he purred slickly as he dropped to his knees behind her. "Can I join in?" Not caring if Erik objected or not, he pulled himself onto Erik's legs, sitting on them as he lifted Carolanne by the hips and guided himself along Erik's shaft inside of her.

She screamed in pure pleasure at the erotically painful sensation of having two men sharing her at the same time.

"Holy shit!" Erik exclaimed, feeling Christopher's hardness rubbing along his, inching him closer to climax. He reached up, grabbed Carolanne's hair, and pulled her close. As they climaxed, Christopher grabbed her, pulling her throat from Erik before he could drink, leaving only her wrist to Erik's hunger, saving the rest for himself.

"My, God…" Christopher moaned as he bit down on Carolanne, feeding on her orgasm as well.

She slammed against them a few times before finally going limp on top of Erik.

~ ~ * ~ ~

"Now that was fun," Christopher said, still grinning. "Just like the good ol' days."

"Yea, I guess. You're still a greedy bastard." Erik looked away.

"What?"

"I dunno. I mean, it was good and all, but…" Erik's voice was low, quiet.

"Out with it."

"She's no Cyn."

"She is a hot lil' number." Christopher licked his lips, still tasting the last bits of blood.

"Hot is right and you've only had a taste of her temper. She cold cocked Lyndsay."

"And she's still alive?" Christopher asked with a shocked laugh.

"Actually, Lyndsay just laughed."

"Good ol' Lyndsay. How's she been?"

"Moody."

"Bad ol' Nick. Hehe, speaking of moody, did ya notice how Cynthia took the car and left us to fend for ourselves?"

"Hey, her kill, her car."

"At least we found a way to amuse ourselves."

"But what now?"

Christopher reached into his pocket and pulled out a deck of cards. "Poker?"

"If she'll let me." Erik laughed.

"Not if I can help it." He handed the deck to Erik.

"Wanna bet?"

"Shut up and deal."

Awakenings: The Wrath Saga

About the Author

Will Van Stone Jr. is the author of Action novella *Stormfront - The Three: The Death Dealer* for which a sequel is imminent. He is the creator of the weekly column, THE BLACK BOOK, which is based entirely on his personal experiences as well as the secrets of his numerous friends (a few of whom have become enemies). Singularly, he is currently working on LE FEY, a new take on the Arthurian Legend. Will currently resides in Ansonia, Connecticut, with his 25 lb cat Fat Madison.

About the Author

S.I. Hayes is the author of The *In Dreams* Fantasy Series. As well as her website and blogs, where she shares just what it's like inside her head, including poetry, novels running awry, and the struggle of being a Bi-Polar writer. Singularly she is working on *Centuries of Blood,* a Vampire Romance novel set in the Wrath Universe that follows the life of one not tied to the Clan. Shannon lives in Ansonia Connecticut.

LOVE YOU TO DEATH

by

Cinsearae S.

Why is it that the things we know are bad for us are the things we crave the most? What is it about the dark side that tempts us? Why is evil so enticing, so alluring, so seductive? The darkness sucks us in like the silly little sheep we can be sometimes, and do we care? Of course not. Although there may be a nagging thought way back in the very depths of our brains, telling us to stop, our flesh and our egos demand otherwise. They desire the "now," the instant gratification, immediate satisfaction, without a second thought to the repercussions of our folly. We can only regret the aftermath, loathe ourselves for our weaknesses we continue to deny, and secretly await the moment we can get that next unhealthy fix, like a heroin addict feeling the pains of withdrawal.

I swore I'd never fall a victim to my own selfish needs, then I found myself a prisoner of my own desires not too long after. To say I had been prudent all my life would be laughable. Try as I might, my relationships with immature men wound up making me jaded, disgusted, disappointed and even hateful of the opposite sex. Intercourse was either self-serving on their end or banal on mine. Connecting with someone seemed pointless in this day and age; everyone was egocentric to the point where I felt like I was talking to a bunch of empty holes and blank slates. You can always tell when someone isn't interested in your conversation; they'll have a very far-away look in their eyes or say "um-hm" a lot. Then, there were the ones who never let you get a word in edgewise, as the topic of conversation was always about themselves. These were the ones that made *you* get that far-away look and say um-hm all the time.

By the time I turned thirty, I was finished with swimming through the dating pool. It was way too stagnant, as far as I was concerned. If I hadn't found a suitable partner by now, I knew I wouldn't find one in the next few months or years. Has anyone really taken a good look at how people behave towards one another lately? All those people with their delusions of grandeur...I'd be better off getting a pet and calling it a day.

No longer worried about trying to make an impression on anybody, I devoted more time to my hobby of photography. Cemeteries were usually my main subject, and I especially loved taking shots during foggy days and twilight times. The lack of people and peacefulness were also a big plus.

I was snapping a few evening shots around a particular crypt that was erected in the early nineteen hundreds: a pristine, mini mansion for the dead. Creeping ivy snaked its way up the walls and around the entrance. I walked up the steps, peeked through the barred window, and noticed six marbled final resting places in the middle of the cramped floor The lid was removed off of one of them. I shoved my camera lens through the bars and snapped a few photos, then ran back down the steps, always worried that some old caretaker would spot me and shoo me away or call the cops.

The crypt had piqued my interest, staying on my mind as I walked. I had only gotten a few yards before I turned to look back at it. The moon gave an eerie bluish-white glow to all the white tombstones and crypts, the dark leafless trees looking like desiccated black claws reaching for the sky. It was creepy and thrilling, yet serene and calming, and at that moment, I realized how much I loved the eeriness of the night.

Screw it. I headed back to the crypt to take more pictures. I seriously doubted a caretaker was walking around at that time of night, anyway.

I took a few wide shots of the crypt before going up the steps and peeking into the window again.

The marble lid was back in place.

My heart felt like it had dropped into my stomach as it squeezed. I felt a surge of coldness shoot through my body until it reached my feet. It had been mere minutes, and the crypt was still within sight. I neither saw nor heard anything to make my fight-or-flight instincts kick in.

Then who put the lid back?

I took a few shots anyway, then decided to get the hell out of there. I was in no mood to play Scooby Doo and solve a mystery... or become one.

As I turned, I nearly screamed. Someone drew me close and covered my mouth with his hand. The person felt emaciated; it was almost like being hugged by a bag of bones.

"Do not scream. I will not hurt you," he whispered in my ear before slowly taking his hand away.

I felt his icy cold touch on my face; his face was completely in shadow under the moon's light. It almost appeared as if he had two hollowed-out eye sockets. His jaws were sunken in, his pallor pale and white, almost glowing as much as the tombstones around us. He had jet-black hair; his clothes were tattered, yellowed with age.

Great. I had run into a derelict.

"You scared the shit out of me," I snapped. "And don't follow me either, unless you want me to break your face."

He titled his head to the side, taken aback. "I will not hurt you," he repeated, his voice sounding softer and... lonely. For a split second, I almost felt bad for him.

"Sorry," I said, dropping my defenses a notch, taking a slow, cautious step back to make my getaway. "You just creeped me out a bit. I'll be on my way."

"Don't go," he pleaded in the same, sad-sounding tone, reaching a hand out to me. "Stay with me."

Was he *nuts*? Hanging out with the homeless was not high on my to-do list. Sometimes, the ones I ran into could be more pushy and violent than the average person.

"Um, sorry, but, I have somewhere to go."

He raised his hand and wiggled his index finger from side to side as if to say, "Liar, liar, pants on fire." Then he beckoned me towards the crypt entrance. What the hell...?

The gated door was unlocked. He pulled it open, the pushed the marbled door forward. My jaw dropped. No way. Was he *sleeping* in there?

Still, I couldn't see him putting that marble lid back on all by himself. Something like that was far too heavy for one man to deal with without needing some help.

Considering I never had anything this interesting happen to me, I warily followed in after him, a single white candle alight in the crypt, casting shadows in the tiny space. One thing was for sure, he moved lightning fast and was as silent as the dead for him to have done that without me knowing.

As he stood in front of the coffins, he spread his arms, gesturing to everything around us as if to say, "Well, this is it." His eyes were heavy with fatigue and sadness, as if the world had shit on him several times over, and now he was reduced to living in a crypt.

"Jesus," I whispered, my voice sounding hollow and closed in. The acoustics in this tiny place were very weird. "I'm so sorry."

He shrugged his shoulders slightly, then sat down in a cobwebbed corner. Although I felt it was impolite to the deceased, I hopped on top of the coffin with the formerly removed lid. "You don't mind, do you?" I asked. He shook his head.

He definitely wasn't one for conversation, so I went first.

"What happened to you? Are you a victim of our shitty economy? Lost a job? Lost your home?"

He gave a faint nod.

"How long have you lived in this crypt?"

"One hundred and five years," he whispered, and I raised my eyebrow. He had to have been a bit delusional, probably from the lack of food. He must have meant four years. I kept going.

"What about family? A wife? Kids?"

"Dead," he replied in the same manner. "No one to love."

Feeling worse for this total stranger, he pointed to the coffins, and I got a funny feeling in the pit of my stomach again.

I slowly slid off the coffin. "What? Are you telling me…?" I looked at the marble caskets, reading the names on each one. "This… this isn't… *your family*, is it?"

He lifted his head, resting it against the wall. "No one to love," he repeated. "All are cold."

His style of verbiage --or lack of--was creeping me out again. He heaved himself up and I tried my best not to run like a terrified rabbit. He walked to the crypt on the far right and put a pale hand on the icy stone, lightly brushing his fingers over the name. "Mother," he began, then moved to the next one, repeating his actions. "Father," he continued. Walking past me, he went to the first one from the left. "Wife," he said, then passed over the one I had sat on to get to the next one. "Son," he said in a soft voice, and then lastly, "Daughter."

There was a bit of silence between us, making me feel tense and uncomfortable. He stood a mere couple of feet from me, looking exhausted. I noticed his eye color was black, something I had never seen before. I summoned up some more courage as I turned my back to him and looked at the crypt in front of me, truly afraid to ask, "Well… who's in this one?"

He came up from behind, placing his dirt-encrusted hands on either side of me, on the coffin's lid. I swallowed.

"Me," he whispered in my ear, then kissed my jaw line.

My heart was racing. This guy was crazy. He *had* to be. And I was stuck in a *very* dangerous situation. Should I fight like a rabid jackal, or keep it calm and collected as I made a getaway?

"Look," I began, still not facing him, but staring at "his" coffin lid. "I'm sure you're speaking metaphorically; I mean, from what you've told me, you've been through hell. Maybe I can help you somehow."

I felt him move away, and I was relieved. But what he did next took me by absolute surprise.

He removed the lid to the coffin on my left like he was opening a shoebox, sliding it to the side and laying it against the crypt with a stony, heavy thunk. A dusty, skeletal corpse wearing the tatters of a dress resided inside. The lining was stained in brown and yellow. Speechless, I backed away. He did the same to his son's coffin, the tiny remains of a little boy probably no older than five peering back at me.

"Need I open more?" he asked in his calm, monotone voice. Feverishly, I shook my head no.

Still, I was confused. The clothing I saw on the corpses looked very… dated. So did his. His wife and children died in 1908; his parents ten years before that. I looked at his coffin lid. He, too, died the same year as his family, and all of them in the same month.

"Cholera," he answered, as if reading the forming question in my mind.

"Dear God," I whispered to myself, staring at him in wonder. The look in his eyes seemed more desperate this time, but for what, I still had no clue. Never mind the fact that this person standing before me should have been one hundred and five years in his grave, but was somehow *alive*. Oddly enough, I was more fascinated than horrified at the scenario before me.

"How are you still *living*?" My skin felt clammy and damp with nervousness.

He paused a long time before answering me, staring at the corpses in their coffins. "Curse," he replied in that whispered, raspy voice of his.

I began to feel as if I were in the middle of a horror story. "A... curse?"

He lowered his gaze, sounding remorseful. "Something... came to me... on my death bed. Promised me life... for a price. It took the last of mine, giving me a new one while stealing my soul. When I asked it to save my family, it told me they were already dead. And now, I walk the night, taking lives to sustain mine." He shook his head. "So tired."

I had a hard time wrapping my head around this. He sounded like the one monster Hollywood has glamorized for ages, and he was nothing of the sort. He was bedraggled, rueful, penniless, and alone. A vagrant of the undead, wishing for death, but unable to have it.

His head snapped up, looking at me. "You did not run."

I shook myself out of my stupor. "What?"

"I have tried approaching a few... in friendship only. They ran. You didn't."

I sniffed, feeling silly. "I guess I did."

He took my hand in his. He was so bony and cold, like he'd sat in a refrigerator all day. "Stay? Talk with me?"

I was now exposed to the most incredulous secret ever. How could I leave?

"Yes, I'll stay and talk with you," I answered, feeling very surreal. Was this really happening?

He opened his arms, beckoning me to him. Still feeling out-of-it, I wrapped my arms around his frail waist, leaning into his hard and bony chest. Wrapping his arms around me, I felt encased in a chill I couldn't shake.

"So warm," he said woefully as he stroked the back of my hair. "How I wish I could be like you."

I looked up at him. "Are you trying to starve yourself to death?" I paused. *Re-death*? I thought to myself.

When he nodded, my heart sank. "Tired of feeding, taking others' lives for my own. Living alone in darkness is not having a true life."

"I don't want you to be alone," I said, placing a hand on his icy chest.

He caressed my face with one hand, and tried to muster a smile. "You are kind, but I could not ask you for more."

"I could visit you," I suggested quickly. "Keep you company."

"How long would you do this before you grew tired of me? I would rue the day that you did not show, to be left in loneliness again." He pulled away, as if he regretted embracing me. "I would not be able to take it."

"I swear to it," I said firmly before my eyes lit up. "Or even better... you could stay with me."

He tried to smile again. "You are very generous, but I do not belong in your world. I belong here."

"Then I'll continue to visit you every night. Promise."

He gave a single nod. "As you wish."

Before I knew it, our lips touched. His were dry and cold like the rest of his body, but offered such a tenderness I had never felt before with any *living* guy. Did it actually take someone having to be undead in order to express real affection?

When he kissed my neck, I thought I felt his teeth graze my skin, and I shivered.

"Never worry," he said, gently brushing my hair away from my face. "I will never take your life, unless you ask to be with me forever."

I nodded, and we held hands for a moment before I left his crypt, heading home. I had way too much on my mind now than wondering about what pictures to shoot tomorrow.

Not only was I in the weirdest situation imaginable, my conscience was screaming at me that this would not fare well for me.

My mind was buzzing. I couldn't sleep all night. All I thought of was the mysterious undead man living in a crypt in a cemetery not far from where I lived.

An undead man. Not a zombie. Those things were the "living dead" and couldn't speak coherently. Still, he was part of the "dead" family, and I would be keeping him company.

Boy, did that sound ridiculous. How long would it be before we became more than friends? What if... he wanted us to become lovers? I shivered at the notion. Pseudo-necrophilia was also not high on my to-do list. It would be like making love to a skeleton. I mean, he looked *really* bad. He was dead serious (pardon the pun) about starving himself to death.

Did he want me to keep him company until he died (again)? If that was the case, then it wouldn't be fair to me. Just after this first encounter, I found myself liking him. Not romantically, but he was like me. Alone. Sad. Wishing for the right one to show up one day.

I didn't want him to die.

I wanted him to be with me.

Are you psycho?! My inner-voice screamed at me. *Are you, really, really **that** desperate that you'll date a dead guy?!*

"A dead guy who still has feelings," I said to myself. "A dead guy who craves a connection with another person again."

~ ~ * ~ ~

When twilight fell and the world had settled down for the night, I made my way back to the cemetery, down the narrow twisted roads and under the equally twisted and gnarled branches of the trees that lined those roads. Not another living soul was in sight. A few crows flew from branch to branch, giving off their loud, brackish caws.

I was feeling lightheaded as my heart pounded. I took deep breaths, trying to calm myself down. What in hell was I doing?!

I knew exactly what I was doing, and I didn't care. I didn't *want* to care. I was willingly playing the stupid card. But right then, it didn't seem stupid to me. I had my reasons for doing this.

Going up the crypt steps and peeking through the tiny window, I saw the lid on his coffin was removed again, his final resting bed empty. He was probably wandering around. Maybe he thought I wouldn't return.

I sighed and turned, about to make my way back down the steps when I gasped and slapped a hand over my mouth. He was standing at the bottom, looking up at me with a surprised expression on his face, head tilted to the side in curiosity.

"You came back," he said, his lips, cheeks, and chin smeared with dried blood.

Dizziness was starting to overpower me. Fearing I would faint if I opened my mouth to speak, I simply pointed at him.

"Animals," he said plainly. "Dead humans would draw too much attention and cause panic."

I composed myself before speaking. "I thought you were trying to starve yourself to death."

He paused…and did I see the slightest hint of a smile? "I thought if I am to have company now, I need to be presentable."

I gave him a second look. I had no clue how many animals he ate before I got there, but their sustenance made him look a hell of a lot better than he did the previous night. He was much more fleshed out, and there was only a trace of his ribs showing under his skin.

"You look…better," I said in a chipper, positive-sounding voice. He grinned.

"Thank you." He held out his hand, inviting me to take it. He wasn't as cold as he was before, either.

We walked around the cemetery, enjoying the moonlight, the crispness of the fall air, and getting to know more about one another. He was fascinated with our current times as much as I was learning about his past. And both of us had a genuine curiosity about what death *truly* meant. He wondered where his family was, if their souls were in a better place, and where his own went when the being who stole it exchanged it for the existence he had now.

Every now and again, I'd catch him stealing glances of me. I said nothing about it at first, but the more he did it, the more nervous I became. He said he wouldn't hurt me, but he was still a creature of darkness. When he did it for the fifth time, I turned and looked at him.

"What is it?" he asked me.

"You keep staring at me." I gave a half-smile so I wouldn't seem too defensive.

He reached out a pallid hand and caressed my cheek. "I'm sorry. It's because... you're beautiful."

I snorted, and he looked taken aback.

"Please don't laugh. Humans take so many things for granted. Being what I am, I can appreciate all the things I cannot have now, and loathe the fact I never took the time to cherish them while living. Humans truly do not know how to live... until they are about to die."

I paused. He made a lot of sense in that statement.

"When morning approaches and I start to see the sun peering over the horizon, I shudder in my cold, dank crypt as the tops of trees begin to reflect the daylight, showing their colors. I've passed by many rose gardens without giving them so much as a second glance. I've listened to the warbling of birds, sometimes wishing they'd quiet their noise. I now only see blackness and hear nothing but crickets when I leave my confines at night." He paused. "There is much to be grateful for, but humans lose sight of what those things are. Many humans die with several regrets looming over their heads."

He looked at me again. "You're different," he continued. "You like to capture moments in time with photographs." He smiled. "Little instants from the past, frozen on a piece of paper."

"People rarely touch paper images now. Everything has become digital."

He wrinkled his nose. "From all you've told me, these digital devices you speak of seem the things of fiction. So much has been made intangible through means of electronic devices. Some things never exchange hands anymore. Humans rely too heavily on electricity. If there was no more of it, where would your society be? Things would come to a grinding halt." This time, he snorted. "You've crippled yourself with your own progress." He looked to the sky. "Mankind has become a beautiful tragedy."

He turned to me again. "I'm sorry. We should speak of better things."

I grinned. "You've done most of the talking tonight," I said. "But I like listening to you. You don't talk the way most men do today."

"I take it that this is a good thing."

I nodded. Though he spoke of depressing stuff, the manner in which he spoke them sounded so proper, so romantic. "Sometimes, I feel like I was born in the wrong era," I continued. "The world was less polluted, less damaged, less tainted by population. Things were more green and beautiful back then." I grinned again. "I even love the style of dress men and women wore back then."

"I must confess the clothing of your time lacks a certain appeal. The women of today wear attire absent of modesty and elegance. Even the men look dull and insignificant."

"Welcome to my world," I said snidely. "Where people mean nothing and technology is everything."

"Why does life move in such a hurried pace? Your modes of transportation are so quick that they pose a danger to pedestrians. People regard each other with disdain, apprehension, contempt, or distrust. I'll admit that these attitudes are no different than they were in my time, but, people today express it so....openly. They act like puerile *beasts* towards one another."

"Chivalry and compassion have long since died," I answered. "Don't ask me what happened to the human race; I'm just as baffled as you are."

He took my hand and squeezed it. "You have become my link to the outside world, my window into the ways of man. Simply watching from afar has not been enough to know what I need to know."

"You mean to tell me you've never left these grounds? Ever?"

"I sleep for years at a time. Sometimes, I awaken for reasons unknown, and when I do, I roam this place, feed on whatever living creatures I find, then stay awake for a few nights out of sheer curiosity as to how much the world has changed, but then go back to sleep for several years again. Each time I've found it less to my liking." He looked at me. "But meeting you…talking to you…has given me a reason to stay awake. To learn. To feel. To love." He put his other hand on top of mine. "Having only yourself for company tends to get… wearisome."

He was definitely right about that.

He caressed my cheek, giving a faint smile. "Can I kiss you again?"

I nodded, and he leaned into to me. Our lips touched, and his were much softer than they were the night before. His skin still felt cool, but I ignored it as my heart raced with the excitement of it all once more.

I saw a faint trace of orange in the horizon. Damn it. Night was over already?

Slowly, he pulled away. "I shall see you tomorrow night, then?"

"Of course." Reluctantly, we let go, silently saying goodbye using just our eyes.

The next two nights were like this; lots of conversation, and more handholding, more caressing, more skin to skin contact with longer embraces. Each night, he looked more human than the last, less cold to the touch. I almost forget what he was. If it weren't for the rags that he wore, no one would have guessed he was a monster. His black eyes stopped bothering me, and his milky white skin held an ethereal beauty to me. Something taboo, forbidden. Actually, to say he was a monster felt wrong. There were many depraved human beings out there that behaved far worse than he ever would.

And the way he'd look at me…there was something sensual and dark behind his stares. Perhaps he was waiting for me to make the first move. The big question was, was I absolutely sure that I wanted it.

On the third night, I decided to do it.

"C'mon. I want to take you to back home to where I live." I took his hand and began to lead him down the path that would take us out of the cemetery.

He stiffened. "I'm not sure that is such a good idea."

"Why not?"

"I've told you before. I don't belong in your world."

"And I don't belong in yours."

"But…you chose to be…."

"And now I'm inviting you into mine."

It was nearing midnight, and there was barely anyone around, which worked in our favor. He would have looked like a derelict to anyone who happened to see him…not that anyone would have cared.

I got him to my home without as much as a blink from passers-by. Walking down the streets with him was actually a little entertaining. He marveled at parked cars, store buildings in the distance, and gawped at the harsh streetlights used to light up neighborhood blocks. Once I got him inside, my nerves calmed down only slightly. The getting-him-home part was over. Now it was the okay-he's-in-my-house-now-what-am-I-gonna-do tension that arose.

I turned on a lamp. He blinked and looked around, those black eyes of his slowly surveying his new surroundings. I watched him move about the living room, silently, cautiously…and it was then that I understood what he meant about not belonging in my world. He was over a century old. A strange man in a strange world. Everything was foreign to him.

He brushed his hands over the entertainment system, his eyebrows furrowed, but not asking any questions. He lightly tapped the television screen, then picked up the remote.

"What kind of device is this?" he asked me.

I smirked. "See that little red button? Push it."

He looked down at the remote, and pushed the button. When the television came on, he dropped the remote and backed away, startled.

"What trickery is this? How are there people speaking to us from within that thing?"

"This is the invention I told you about, called television."

Wide-eyed, he stepped forward and touched the screen again. "A marvel indeed."

"Not really. It could serve much better purposes, but we use it for crap like reality shows."

He paused. "Reality...shows?"

I shook my head. "Never mind. It's not worth even talking about." I took a deep breath and ran a hand through my hair. "Would you like something to drink? I'm sure you get tired of feeding off of animals. Some wine, maybe? You...do drink wine...right?"

"Of course."

Well, that dispelled one myth.

I went into the kitchen, grabbed a bottle, then twisted a corkscrew into the cork, pulling it from the neck, and poured us two glasses. As I turned to leave the kitchen, he was there. I gasped, and he gently took a glass from me.

"Thank you," he said, taking a sip, letting it sit in his mouth for a moment to savor the flavor. He swallowed. "Different from what I'm used to, not that I'm being picky." He smiled and put the glass down on the counter, so I gulped down what I had. I hoped it would ease my nerves, and quick.

He cupped my face in his hands, and I looked into those fathomless black eyes of his. He pulled me in for another kiss.

The temperature in the house must have warmed his body. He didn't feel cold to me anymore. The kiss deepened, our tongues intertwining, every nerve in me tingling as his hands roamed my backside, traveling downward and resting on my buttocks. The wine mellowed me out, making me more receptive to his advances.

"Are you sure this is what you want?" he whispered in my ear. I nodded.

His kisses traveled down my neck and chest, to my cleavage. He unbuttoned my shirt, letting it drop to the floor. He then ripped off what was left of his own, and my hands graced the silky smoothness of his chest, the ruddiness of my skin a stark contrast to his moonlike pallor.

In one swoop, he had picked me up off of my feet, walked through my dining and living rooms, then up my stairs. He found my bedroom, settling us both on the mattress. He fumbled with the zipper on my skirt, not sure how to work it, so I helped him along. Once he removed his pants, we lay there together in near-nakedness.

"You've made me so happy in such a short time," he told me, brushing my hair away from my face. "How I wish this moment could last forever."

"We can *make* it last forever."

"Nothing is forever…but let's make this last for as long as we can."

He looked into my eyes so deeply, I felt as if he touched my soul. Then he ran his fingers down the lines of my body, making me shiver. He cradled me close to him, wrapping his strong arms around my waist, holding me tight, as if he was afraid to let me go. He deepened his kisses once more as I ran my hands across his broad shoulders, relishing every second we had together, every strand of his energy dancing against mine.

I could feel his hardness start to push against my thigh as he caressed my breasts. Mentally, I screamed with the excitement of it all. Every touch was electric, my senses heightened to a level I never felt before.

His kisses traveled downward, past my navel. He planted more kisses on my pelvic bone, giving it a slight nibble, sending tickling sensations across my hips. He parted my thighs, running his tongue across that sensitive inner-flesh, then slowly bit into my femoral artery.

First, there was the initial prick of his fangs, but the rest had me swooning. He suckled me like a hungry babe, his tongue brushing against the fresh wound he made. The feeling sent a streak of hot-white heat straight to my clit, and it began to swell in response. I squirmed at bit, trying to keep control as it started to throb, needing attention.

I arched my back as he began to suckle it as fervently as he did my inner thigh. It twitched against his feathery flicks, slow strokes and gentle pulls, and then his tongue penetrated my tunnel, exploring me, tasting me.

I started panting, gripping the sheets. Within a minute, I was crying out as I saw stars while a river of warmth ran from me. Staring intently in my eyes, he took care of the rest. His manhood gave off an intense heat as I felt the tip of his cock penetrate my folds for the briefest moment before his thickness plunged deep into me in one smooth, hard, stroke. His entire length filled me, stretching my entrance, claiming my womanhood, intensifying that internal fire that demanded his presence. I moaned and closed my eyes, wrapping my legs across his waist, mashing his body to mine, urging him to push his manhood deeper into me.

His thrusts were slow, deliberate, as if cherishing the act. Our closeness hit my very core, our connectedness deepening in a way that transcended mere physicality. I tightened my legs around him, wanting him to melt into me. Our foreheads touched, then his lips met mine again. We expressed our love for one another without saying a single word.

He moaned and slowly gyrated his hips, the sensation of his cock moving around in my tunnel resulting in another explosive reaction from me. My thighs trembled as his thrusts became more intense. He buried his face in my neck, his breath warm against my skin. His fangs pierced my flesh as he drank me in again. The combined sensations I received made me dizzy to the point of wanting to lose consciousness.

He stiffened, the tip of his cock having reached the very depths of me, giving me that deep, pleasure-pain sensation that finally quenched the fire in my core. Tightening my vaginal walls around his shaft, I heard him moan once more as I felt his hardness pulsing in response. When his orgasm ebbed, we basked in the afterglow of our lovemaking, the sheets pulled up over us as we slept under the moon's glow. I never felt so at peace, so comfortable, so secure.

This felt right. I was still a bit unsure as to what the future could possibly bring, but I was prepared to deal with whatever curves fate would throw our way.

When I awoke, it was noon. But instead of having him in my arms, I was cuddling a bunch of pillows. The shades on the windows were drawn, sunlight streaming in. I squinted, my eyes trying to focus.

Abruptly I sat up, looking around. I threw back the sheets and jumped out of bed, running through the house looking for him. My house was as silent as the grave.

Did he go back to his crypt before the sun rose?

Hastily, I threw on a shirt, a pair of yoga pants, a jacket, and stuffed my feet into the pair of sneakers I had placed beside my front door. I took a quick jog down to the cemetery, trying not to panic.

I found his crypt and peeked into the tiny window. The marble slab to his coffin was still in the exact place where he left it, his casket empty.

My heart was pounding. I sat on the crypt steps for a moment, trying to think.

Something told me to go back home.

My entire body was shaking. I stood up, forcing my legs to move. I was feeling nothing but trepidation, and something in me did *not* want to go back to my house.

~ ~ * ~ ~

Placing my keys on the counter, I felt completely numb. My heart was pounding as I took slow, deliberate steps up the stairs and back into my room. I stood in the doorway, surveying everything.

The sunlight was so bright. I looked across my unmade bed to the open bay windows. I crossed the floor, walking towards them.

Why was there a huge scorch mark by the window?

I didn't want my brain to calculate the obvious as I kneeled down and ran my fingers across the mark. My face became hot as the tears began to flow. No. NO. I would not accept this. I *couldn't* accept this, not after everything we spoke of, everything we shared.

My legs finally gave out and I sat on the floor. My brain went "tilt" as I think I stared at that mark for an hour before I came out of my stupor. Running a hand through my hair, I looked to the nightstand, and spotted a piece of paper. I got up on wobbly legs, picked up the piece of paper, and read it.

You've known that for years I shunned human contact, my few attempts unsuccessful. And then you arrive, fearful yet determined, showing me that there is still a glimmer of hope for such a doomed race. You've given me companionship, and the chance to know what it's like to love another again. A creature such as myself couldn't ask for anything more.

You have a way of speaking while being silent. I think that's what I loved the most about you. You spoke to me with every smile you gave me, every time we touched, whenever we would embrace. You have a vibrancy that cannot be compared to the average mortal, and our closeness is something I will always cherish.

It took me over a hundred years to find you, and because we connected, it is why I could not bear to share my curse with you. You give life to a dying world, and it would be selfish of me to keep you to myself, to turn you into something that can only dwell in darkness when your light shines so bright. I'd rather die than have you become like me. My existence was not "living," it was merely torture, and I could not have you partake in such madness. Removing myself from your world permanently was the only solution.

Please do not be angry with me. I did this because the world needs more people like you in it. I did this because I want you to flourish. I did this because I love you.

Do not think of my departure as death, as you've given me peace and made me complete. I can finally leave this world without having any regrets. And in knowing that, I hope you will continue to live out the rest of your life the same way.

I will forever be grateful for knowing you, and I will always remain eternally yours.

I read it quite a few times, my emotions running from angry, to woeful, then to depressed. In my eyes, I felt it was selfish of him to take his love away from me. There would never be another out there like him. He had given me the best days of my life, as short as they were.

But, he knew that eventually I would ask him to make me like him, so he had his reasons for doing what he did. He was trying to protect me, save me from a proverbial hell of desperation and sadness. He did it because he loved me so much that he did not want to see me reflect what he was.

It took me a while to finally accept his decision. But in his eyes, I had saved *him*. Realizing that, I felt a little better. I helped someone. And I hoped with every fiber of my being that he was in a better place.

About the Author

Dark Paranormal Romance/Horror author Cinsearae S. is the creator of *Diary of a Vampire Stripper*, Top 10 Finisher in the Predators & Editors 2012 Readers Polls. A digital artist, jewelry designer, and still-photographer, she is also editor/publisher of award-winning, *Dark GothicResurrected Magazine*. She received the Author's Site of Excellence Award in 2007 from Predators & Editors, and is a cover artist for Damnation Books and independent authors. Her website won a Golden Horror Award from Horrorfind.com. Shop owner of Mistress Rae's Decadent Designs on Etsy.com, (Search: MistressRae13) she specializes in Steampunk, Halloween, Victorian and Gothic-inspired jewelry, accessories, creepy dolls, anthropomorphic oddities, and more. Her store won the 2012 Fright Times Award for "Best Horror Collectible," and was recently featured on WFMZ.com (Channel 69 in Allentown, PA). An avid fan of "old school" horror movies and their villains (Freddy, Jason, Michael, Pinhead) she is also a big Vincent Price fan. Halloween is her favorite time of the year, and she keeps her house decorated year round. She has always been drawn to the flipside of life -- the supernatural, odd, bizarre, Gothic and "darkly beautiful" always being an inspiration to her. She lives with her husband and two rat terriers, aptly named Hades and Chaos. You can also find her on Youtube, Facebook, Pinterest and Twitter.

EVERLASTING HUNGER

An Excerpt

By

Brandy Dorsch

Jasper emerges from the shadows along the back wall, tugging Ellie with him. "That looked like a show we would've put on, gorgeous." He smiles down at her. "I'm hoping that you two will become friends. She's going to be going with us to the masquerade ball and I bet Ian will have her meet you for a fitting as well."

Ellie pulls Jasper around to face her and wraps her arms around his neck. "I think that'll be great, Jasper. I'm looking forward to having a week of fun and distractions."

Jasper growls softly as he nips at the curve of her shoulder. "I think you're distraction enough, gorgeous. Do you want to go see if you can find Ian for some fun? I have to head back up to my office to finish up a few things, but you are welcome to come with me."

Ellie shakes her head. "You have no idea how tempting it is to head to your office with you, handsome. However, I think I'm going to say good night. I still have to pack for my stay up at the cabin and I want to get that done tonight."

She looks around the bar. "Any ideas on where I could find Ian at to say goodbye?"

Jasper grabs her hand and heads across the room to the VIP lounge. "I'm betting that he is in here waiting for you, gorgeous." Kissing her gently at the door, he turns and heads to his office, up the stairs.

Knocking lightly, Ellie enters the VIP lounge and glances around, her eyes drawn to the man sprawled out in sensual abandon on the daybed.

"Hello, my love. I was wondering if I was going to have to kidnap you from Jasper."

Crawling up on the bed and straddling the half-naked vampire, she starts to unbutton his shirt. "I was having a good time and I have to say the show you put on with that beautiful drink was impressive. Most women would be jealous, but I was amazed at the beauty and sensuality of it."

Shrugging out of his shirt and toeing off his shoes, Ian raises up as Ellie unbuttons his pants and pushes them down. "I was hoping that the regular diners would take an interest in her. She is new and was having a difficult time tonight serving drinks."

Ellie gazes in awe at the perfection of the man lying beneath her and starts to kiss and stroke the muscles of his chest. Flicking her tongue against his nipple, she can feel the tremor caused by her touch. Ian threads his hands in her hair as she kisses her way down his body. After circling his navel with her tongue, she slides down to take his erection into her hands. Stroking the silky shaft with her hands, she slowly slips the plum-colored tip between her lips and down the back of her throat.

With her face nestled in the curls between his thighs, Ellie uses her tongue to stroke his thick, hard shaft as she works it in and out of her mouth. Ellie loves the feel of Ian growing harder while she pleasures him. When his body begins to tighten, she rises and impales herself on his cock. Riding him hard, she pulls him up to the curve of her neck and moans aloud as he sinks his fangs in and begins to drink. Clenching her body around his and holding his head to her neck, she explodes just as Ian reaches his peak. Pleasure spreads as his semen pulsates into her womb, and she feels her inner walls contract in time with Ian as he continues to drink.

Ellie strokes his hair softly as he pulls at the vein in her neck. Feeling satisfied from the lovemaking but slightly dizzy, Ellie's hand drops from his head as she begins to grow weaker.

"Ian, I think you need to stop." Ellie tries to pull away from Ian, but she does not have the strength. "Ian, please stop."

Beginning to panic, Ellie pushes at Ian's head, trying to pull him away, but she cries out at the sharp pain from his fangs. With darkness closing in and feeling betrayed by Ian, Ellie gathers all of her strength and screams for the one person she hopes can help. *"Jasper!"*

Knowing that she was too weak for him to hear her, Ellie fades into darkness, knowing that her fear of death was becoming a reality.

Sitting at his desk and trying to get the spreadsheet for the inventory completed, Jasper taps his foot in rhythm to the music in the club below. It had been a fun and interesting night, but Jasper was beginning to have the feeling that something was seriously wrong. Pushing the intercom button on his desk to the main bar, he asks if there are any problems.

"Not that we have been made aware of, sir," says the bartender.

"Thank you," Jasper replies, clicking off the intercom and turning back to the spreadsheet.

Within seconds, he realizes that something is drawing him downstairs and he pushes back from the desk. His instincts have saved him countless times in battle and something tells him that there is a problem with Ian. Heading down the stairs and taking the employee route to the VIP lounge, his heart stops when he hears a weak scream.

"Jasper!"

Taking off at a dead run, he slams open the door to the lounge and sees Ian feeding on an unconscious Ellie. Fearing that he has not made it in time to save her, he rips Ian away from her throat and pulls Ellie to the ground. Hearing feral growls at his back, Jasper turns and flashes his fangs at Ian.

"What is your problem, Ian? Are you trying to kill her?"

When he pulls Ian away from her, he unintentionally rips her throat open, and the blood is pulsating out in rhythm with her slowing heartbeat.

Balling up a sheet and trying to slow the blood, Jasper realizes there is too much damage to her neck to heal her. Normally, after drinking, a vampire would just lick the puncture wounds closed, but these are deep gashes and the vein's exposed. The only way to save her is to feed her vampire blood. "Ian, I need you to come here and help me. Ian?"

Glancing over his shoulder, Jasper sees Ian sitting with his head clasped in his hands. Seeing his shoulders shaking, Jasper can tell he is upset. However, now is not the time.

"Ian, if you want to save her, you need to come over here now!"

Ian looks at him, then pulls himself up

"What did I do, Jasper? I couldn't stop. She tried to push me away and I couldn't stop drinking."

"We'll figure it out at a later time. Right now, we have to save her. I know she doesn't want to die, but that's what is going to happen.

Do you want to change her or do you want me to do it?"

Ian looks from the woman he tried to kill to his best friend, and makes a choice.

"Do it for me, Jasper. I think that there is something wrong with me. I don't feel like my normal self and I'm afraid that I will do her more harm than good."

Jasper inhales sharply. "Do you understand what that means for us? She will be mine as well. You know I have felt a connection to her and she could be a mate for me. Are you willing to accept that?"

Ian looks into eyes that are so similar to his long-dead father's and replies, "Jasper, you are family to me and I'll share anything and anyone with you. This woman is important to us both and, through my actions, we are about to lose her. Save her and I'll give her up if that's her choice."

Jasper pulls the sheet away and sees that the blood is slowing down, but her heartbeat is fading as well. Realizing that there is not much time to waste, he picks Ellie up, wraps her in a blanket, and heads to the rear entrance of the lounge.

"Where are you taking her, Jasper?"

Jasper turns slightly. "Somewhere safe so she can complete her transformation and I can explain all of this to her. Meet Annabelle and the other women here at eleven tomorrow, and explain the situation to them. I'll see you in a few days."

Not saying another word, he heads out the door and down the hall to the elevator. Checking to make sure she is still breathing, he takes the elevator to the parking garage and races to his car. Gently placing her in the passenger seat, he buckles her in and climbs into the driver's seat. Slamming the car into drive, he speeds off the ramp and down the street. Taking the roads and turns as quickly as he can, he turns into a long driveway that disappears into the woods at the edge of the city. Pulling up in front of a large mansion, he hops out and pulls Ellie into his arms, checking to make sure that she is still breathing.

He kicks and bangs on the door until his butler, Dudley, answers. Pushing past him, he rushes up the stairs and places her on the king-sized bed in his room. He pulls his jacket and shirt off and tosses them in the corner of the room.

"Is the young lady ill, my lord?"

Jasper shoves fingers through his hair anxiously. "Yes, Dudley. She was drained tonight and will die if I don't complete the transformation."

Dudley walks in and closes the curtains. "Do you not want to help the young lady, sir?"

Shaking his head, Jasper answers, "It's not that, Dudley. She's a potential Hunger mate for Ian and I've felt the connection to her myself. I don't understand how that's possible, but it's there."

Dudley straightens as his master paces the floor. "I would imagine that you both feel the connection since you are both related, my lord."

Jasper stops his frantic steps and looks at Dudley in astonishment.

"Did you not know that you and Lord Lochlan were blood relatives, my lord?"

"No, I didn't know that, Dudley, but that explains a lot of things and it will have to wait for another time. I need to take care of Ellie before I lose her. Can you bring up a bottle of scotch and a bottle of the component mixture?"

Jasper sits on the edge of the bed and pulls the blanket from around Ellie while he waits for Dudley to bring up the drinks. Seeing how much blood she has lost and feeling how slow her heartbeat is, Jasper knows he's doing the right thing by her. Shaking her gently, he tries to rouse her.

"Ellie, honey. I need you to wake up and look at me. Come on, gorgeous. Flash those sexy blue eyes at me."

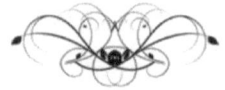

Ellie feels the pull of the darkness and longs to stay there, but she can hear a voice calling to her, pulling at her soul. Heading toward that voice, Ellie slowly opens her eyes and gazes into the sad, hazel eyes of Jasper.

Whispering softly, she says, "What's wrong, Jasper?"

"Gorgeous, I need you to listen to me carefully because we don't have much time. Ian was drinking from you while you were making love. Something happened while he was drinking; he didn't stop and almost drained you. I pulled him off you, but since his fangs were buried, your throat was ripped open. I can save you, honey, but I need to know if you want me to do the transformation."

Looking into her eyes and seeing the panic breaks Jasper's heart and he pulls her into his arms, mindful of the bleeding wound.

"Jasper, I don't want to die. Will you save me?"

Closing his eyes and saying a swift prayer, Jasper leans back against the headboard and tucks her back to his chest. "Ellie, I will always save you. I need you to understand what this means, though. If I transform you, then you are as much mine as I'm yours. I offered to let Ian turn you, but he was afraid that he would not be able to without killing you."

"Jasper, you know that I felt a connection with you. I know what being a vampire means. Love, passion, and forever takes on different meaning when you live centuries. Belonging to you as a mate is not a hardship, but what happens if you find a Hunger mate?"

Feeling her growing weaker, Jasper speeds up the conversation. "My butler, Dudley believes that Ian and I are blood relatives, which would explain how I was able to sense that you needed me from my office. If you are a possible mate for him, it makes sense that you are mine as well. We can figure that all out later, gorgeous. Can I do this now and save your life?"

Closing her eyes, she nods her head. "What do I need to do, Jasper?"

Pulling a Swiss army knife out of his pocket, he opens it and swipes it across his wrist. "Just drink, gorgeous, and I will take care of the rest."

Jasper raises his wrist to her mouth. He can tell she feels weak and is close to death as she swallows the first drops of his blood.

Jasper holds steady as Ellie slowly drinks from his wrist, knowing that she is reliving all of his life memories and sealing the bond that will forever be between them.

Feeling the sizzle of her thoughts merging with his, Jasper knows that he will never be able to just hand her over to Ian. They will have to find a way to make it work. Jasper could sense Ian trying to connect with Ellie, but since she is drinking from Jasper, his hold is stronger, and once they make love, his connection with her thoughts will be solid and Ian's will fade.

Feeling the tug of her lips on his wrist, Jasper glances down and realizes that her wound is starting to close up. His thoughts are interrupted by a knock on the door.

"Come in, Dudley."

Walking in and placing the drinks on a small table near the window, Dudley turns to Jasper.

"My lord, I've been with you for a long time, and I feel like I need to say something to you."

Sighing because he knows the old man thinks of him as a son, Jasper asks, "What is it?"

"I have known for some time now that Lord Ian was a blood relation. When I learned this, I should've brought it to your attention. However, I was under the assumption that sometime in the last four centuries, he would've made mention of it. I'm sorry for not telling you about it sooner."

Shrugging slightly so as not to dislodge Ellie from her resting place, he replies, "It's fine, Dudley. These things have a way of working themselves out."

Bowing to the couple on the bed, Dudley turns and walks out of the room, shutting the door behind him.

Beginning to feel slightly lethargic, Jasper checks the wound on Ellie's neck and sees that it's almost completely closed. Feeling the strength of her heartbeat returning, he smiles, since he knows she is on the mend and beginning the transformation. Pulling on his wrist, he attempts to dislodge Ellie from her drinking, only to have her latch on ferociously.

"Ellie, love, you have to let me go now so we can finish."

She opens her dazzling blue eyes and slowly releases her grip on his arm.

"Jasper? What's going on? Where am I?"

Jasper rises from the bed and heads to the table with the drinks. Pouring a double for himself, he mixes a blood cocktail for Ellie and hands it to her.

"Sweetheart, I did the only thing that I could and that was to transform you. Ian ripped a chunk of your neck out when I pulled him off you. We're at my house and I fed my blood to you. Can you ever forgive me?"

She smiles a breathtaking smile up at him. "You saved me and the transformation seems very simple to me."

Jasper shakes his head. "It's not complete yet, Ellie. Go ahead and drink that cocktail and I will explain what is going to happen next."

About the Author

Brandy Dorsch lives in North Dakota and dreams of running away and being an extra on *The Vampire Diaries*. She is a diehard reader that can't breathe without adding something to her TBR list. She loves anything romance, but has a special place in her heart for all things vampire related. She works and goes to school, but her favorite activity is spending time with her husband and two sons. She recently released her debut novel, *Everlasting Hunger* and has two more WIPs coming soon!

DOUBLE THE SIN

Sinners 3.5

An erotic "SINNERS" short

By

Charity Parkerson

About the story:

After a vicious attack by a creature of the night, Annie James loses not only her ability to walk in the sunlight but also the man of her dreams, Adio.

Adio's guilt over his failure to keep Annie safe has kept him at a distance, and although he has kept a close watch on her since her turning, he has made no attempt to reclaim the love they once shared...until now.

☾ ☆ ☾ ☆ ☾ ☆ ☾ ☆ ☾

"God bless the Wal-mart and their twenty-four hour service," Annie thought as she wandered the surprisingly busy aisles at nine o'clock at night. Too few places accommodated the vampire lifestyle. Luckily, in the wintertime, sunset came early and she was able to visit the mall, but during the summer, she missed everything.

363

It was not that she needed anything. It was more like she could not stand the silence of the night. It was lonely and the memories of her time with Adio always seemed to storm her brain once the darkness settled in. He had almost always came to her in the night. As a matter of fact, they fought about it quite often, but when they would make up afterwards, it was oh-so-hot. Six months ago, her life changed dramatically when her boss, Narmer Horus, had presented her with an all-expense-paid trip to Vegas for the weekend. Adio worked as Mr. Horus' driver, and Annie had tried to convince him to join her, but he insisted that their boss needed him. When she returned from her trip to the house where she lived and worked as a personal assistant, she found it completely devoid of life. Narmer, his grown daughter Kim, and most importantly, Adio, were gone. Somehow, she had always known the day would come when they would leave her behind, but for some reason, she had not expected it to be so abrupt. Perhaps she'd envisioned they would give her a choice in the matter and that she would die of old age while in their service. Her mind and heart had screamed in denial as she aimlessly wandered outside to her car. She had not known where she would go, but it turned out not to matter, because she never made it back to her vehicle. The world had gone black and when she awoke, she learned that even though she had believed that there was nothing left to lose, she had been wrong. She did not remember much about the attack itself, but the result was an eternal life cursed to the darkness, and no Adio to ease the burden of it.

☾ ☆ ☾ ☆ ☾ ☆ ☾ ☆ ☾

She smiled brightly at the woman who was stocking shelves as she passed, but her eyes held a deep sadness that was breaking his heart. He continued to watch as she stared at the scented candles in front of her, seemingly lost in thought. She lifted her hand to her mouth and absently brushed the pad of her finger over her bottom lip.

He had never truly understood the power another person could hold over him until he met her. He had never understood the power of a kiss either, until no one kissed him any longer. The phantom feeling of her lips brushing his sometimes made him feel as if he was going insane. It settled into the center of his chest and made his limbs feel heavy as he moved in her direction. She had not been ignorant of their species. She had known from the very beginning, but he had never wanted this life for her. After the attack and turning, he could feel her anger and pain. She had every right to it. They were the ones who brought this awful curse into her life, and he wished like hell that she had never met them, but he could no longer stay away.

She needed to remember never to come to this store on a Friday night at nine p.m. again. The aisle was packed with people and the flow of foot traffic was hindered by an older red-haired lady who was scanning items with some sort of handheld scanner. A chill brushed over Annie's skin, making her feel as if someone was watching her. She lifted her eyes from the row of gingerbread-scented candles in front of her, and a ringing began in her ears as her heart skipped a beat in her chest. The crowd parted like the Red Sea, but it did not matter, since he stood a good foot taller than everyone else. Although this scene had played out several times in her mind over the past months, her reaction was not what she would have expected. In her mind, she envisioned her perfect snub, but instead she stood frozen like a deer in headlights. No matter that, her brain screamed for her to run, hide, or even spit in his face, but all she could do was stare at him. He was every bit as gorgeous as she remembered.

A part of her knew that nothing was wrong with her memory, but another part of her continued to hope that she had only built him up in her mind. It was not to be. His tall muscular frame, combined with his exotic look, caused every girl that he passed to take a second glance. Of course, his chocolate-brown eyes, wavy black hair, and full bottom lip helped him land her back when they first met. The tiny black tattoos etched beneath each of his eyes added an edge of danger to him that made him seem absolutely irresistible. Despite all the things that he was unleashing on the unsuspecting women around them, Annie could not help the possessiveness that welled up inside of her. Adio was hers. It did not matter that he was gone from her life, because her heart belonged to him. He would always belong to her. Tears welled in her eyes and her nose stung at that thought. She was tainted now and he was not. He could bask in the sunlight and hold onto that perfect Egyptian skin tone that he was born with, while she could now only bathe herself in the moonlight. She felt he was a world away and a lifetime ago, even as the memory of their nights together burned brightly in her mind every second of each day. He had always been like an exotic animal to her. He was beautiful to the point that she wanted to touch him, but he was dangerous, and could possibly rip her to shreds. Perhaps that was half his appeal. He did not stop moving until he was mere inches from her and she was forced to tilt her head back in order to look into his eyes.

"Son of a bitch," she said under her breath. Why did he have to be perfect in every way?

His face remained impassive. "Annie," he said stoically.

Bastard. "Adio," she said in return, and damned if his name did not sound like "bastard" as it fell from her lips. He smiled, *fucking smiled*, as if he found her humorous, and a nearby woman sighed at the sight. Annie wanted to stomp his toes, knee him in the balls, and then she wanted to cry because he was so fucking perfect.

His smile fell when she did not return it. "I've missed you," he told her softly.

"Bastard," she hissed before she could stop herself.

The older lady who was stocking the shelves chimed in. "Honey, that's no way to talk to a man that fine."

Annie's head snapped around so fast it almost made her dizzy. "You have no idea what he's done," she hissed at the unsuspecting woman.

The woman, who had been on her knees working, slowly stood, brushing off her jeans as she went. She placed her scanning gun on the shelf and then leaned her elbows upon it, giving Annie her full attention. "Well, I've got four more hours on the clock. I'm all ears."

Annie noticed that several other customers lingered nearby, straining their necks and obviously hanging on their every word. Fine, she thought bitterly. She would give them the gossip they sought.

"He left me when I needed him the most," she answered, and at the same time Adio said, "I failed to keep her safe." Shocked by his words, Annie spun back around and stared into his eyes. Vaguely, she registered the words of the woman behind her.

"Ah, I see. An unplanned pregnancy and he ran out on you. You're right, honey. He is a bastard." A beeping noise began signaling the woman's return to her work, and the volume of the crowd around them increased as they all moved away, satisfied with their new bit of gossip. Annie did not care about any of that. He thought that he had failed her. Well, he was right. She had been scared, alone, and with powers that she had no idea how to control. She had never been so goddamn disappointed by anyone in her entire life as she was in the man who stood in front of her now. Yes, he still held her heart and he always would, but she did not have to let him stomp on it ever again.

"I have to go," she heard herself say, and her feet began to move before her mind even registered the motion. Her feet were smart, she realized. They knew that the rest of her was weak.

Stunned by her words, Adio almost allowed her to pass without reacting, but at the last second, he snagged her arm before she could get away. She froze in her tracks and a look of shock passed over her face, but she made no move to pull away. A million things ran through his head that he wanted to say, but instead, he pulled her into his arms and covered her mouth, uncaring of their surroundings.

It did not matter if a hundred people were watching. They all ceased to exist the moment Adio's lips touched hers. No one could make the world fall away the way that she could. He did not know who the first to pull away was, but neither one of them seemed to want it to end. Their parted lips barely touched as, with eyes closed, they simply breathed each other's air. He wanted all of her, even the air from her lungs. These moments were more erotic to Adio than the most passion-filled caresses, and these were the moments that he had missed the most. It would sneak up on him when he least expected it and rip his heart to shreds. It happened sometimes when he was doing the most mundane things. One moment his focus would be on all the events of the day, and suddenly her face would appear, leaving him breathless. Nothing had changed, he realized suddenly, and it never would.

He pulled away slightly, staring down at her upturned face. She kept her eyes closed and he could see her struggling to catch her breath. "Do you hear that?" she whispered.

Since Adio had lost the ability to focus on anything other than her the moment their lips met, he had not heard a thing. "What?" he asked, and she slowly opened her eyes.

"The sound of the final piece of my heart breaking," she answered as she pushed away from him. He watched her walk away without a clue as to what he should do next. It was not that he thought that she would fall into his arms and forgive him his transgressions. However, he had hoped that she knew him well enough to know that he had not left her to fend for herself all these months.

"Funny, you don't look stupid."

Adio turned and raised a questioning brow at the woman who was stocking shelves. He had forgotten all about her, but he could not let a comment like that one pass without challenge. "Are you questioning my intelligence?"

She shrugged, not appearing cowed by him in the least. "If you don't go after her, then yeah, I am. A girl doesn't let a man kiss her like that and then run away, unless she wants to be chased." When he did not immediately react to her words, she added. "Why are you still standing here?"

Spurred more by hope than the woman's words, he set out to win back his woman.

Annie waited until she was completely hidden from sight in order to shift. She could hear her bones crack and a feeling of weightlessness overcame her as she took to the skies. Her white feathers shined brightly against the dark sky. Thankfully, Kim had sent someone out in search of Annie shortly after Kim's father had left Annie in the woods and on her own. Annie shuddered to think what would have happened to her the first time she shifted, without the guidance of Cherish Anderson, another immortal with the ability to fly. Cherish had taken Annie under her wing, literally, and saved her afterlife. Now Annie could soar through the skies and survive on her own. If only she could out-fly her need for Adio.

Her tiny apartment was the perfect size for her, but the best thing about it was its location. With her patio door facing a tree line and hidden from sight, it allowed her to shift directly at her door. However, tonight, she knew as soon as she opened the door that she was not alone.

She also knew, without having to look, that Adio was standing in the darkness of her living room. Instead of playing a coy game of why-did-you-show-up-here, she skipped the niceties and went straight for the heart of the matter, since she knew that she might never get the chance again to tell him how he had hurt her.

"You never came to look for me, and Narmer left me all alone in the middle of the woods. I had no clue of what I would become. Why didn't he stay and help me? Why didn't he tell me what it would be like to be like him?"

Adio did not attempt to deny her accusations. "Narmer left to keep you safe. He's dangerous. Narmer couldn't tell you what it would be like because he is a different beast. Narmer is an immortal who was bitten by a cursed god in beast form. Those two powerful bloodlines created an unexpected monster. You were born human and turned by the taint. Did you not wonder why you turned into a bird and not a wildcat like the one that turned you?"

"I did, but Cherish explained it to me. She said it was unique to each person. That it depended upon your personal animal instinct and personality." Annie paused before adding, "I don't know what I would have done if Cherish had not come for me. She really understood everything that I was feeling."

"Why do you think that I chose her?" Adio asked.

"*You* chose her?" Annie repeated in disbelief.

"Yes."

"Then you did know where I was all along and you still chose to stay away," she accused.

"I couldn't stand the thought of seeing the hatred in your eyes that I knew you must be feeling towards me. I was supposed to keep you safe, but instead, I sent you away and left you open to attack. You'll never know how much I have tortured myself over that decision."

"Why did you come back?" The whispered question fell from Annie's lips before she could stop herself, but she needed to know. She needed to hear him say the words and set her free.

Adio glanced away before quietly answering. "I become a little less every day without you."

Annie's breath caught in her throat at his words. She knew exactly what he meant. She became a little less each day too. Every day that thing inside of her, that made her the person that she was, faded away without him.

Adio moved until he stood toe to toe with Annie and he cupped her chin in his hand forcing her eyes to meet his. "Say that you will forgive me," he cajoled. "Let me remind you of who you are and what we are together." A second later, Adio appeared behind her, lightly kissing the nape of her neck. Her eyes fell closed at first brush of his lips as the memory of their nights together flooded her brain. They had played this game often. Adio was an *asha*. He could become as many people as he wanted to be at one time, and many nights he had overwhelmed her senses with this second version himself that she had loving dubbed as "Mirage."

"That's not fair," she whispered as Mirage began removing her clothes. Despite her weak protest, he did not stop, and she did not bring his motions to a halt.

"Love seldom is," Adio retorted as the final item of her clothing disappeared from sight. Burying his fingers in her hair, Mirage tugged, tilting her head back so that he could cover her mouth with his own. His tongue invaded her mouth without mercy while Adio focused his attention on her breasts. He nipped at each one until she began to squirm and then he dropped to his knees. He lifted her leg over his shoulder and sealed his mouth over her dripping wet pussy. In an attempt to stay upright, Annie leaned further into the solid wall of Mirage's chest as the pleasure nearly brought her to the floor. Grabbing her hands, Mirage brought them upwards to her own breast urging her to massage them as he kept her hands trapped beneath his. Adio's tongue continued to probe lightly at her folds coming close to where she needed him most, but never giving it to her. She dug her heel into his back and rocked her hips against him, attempting to take what she wanted from him, but the harder she worked the lighter his touch became as he teased her into a frenzy. Mirage kept her mouth busy with his, drowning out all of her moans. Adio flicked his tongue softly over her clit and buried two fingers inside of her. He slid them in and out before using her cream to ease the entry into her ass, causing her to nip at Mirage's bottom lip. She could feel her own juices sliding down her inner thigh and Adio tried to catch every drop with his mouth. Her mind and her body were both screaming with need until she thought that she would snap. Finally, Adio gave into her cries and sucked her clit between his teeth, sending her over the edge. Her muscles shook with the force of her orgasm and Mirage swallowed her screams. She barely registered her foot touching the floor as Mirage was now fully supporting her weight. Mirage slowly lifted his head and she opened her eyes, feeling a bit dazed. The look in his chocolate gaze made her thankful that he was holding her upright. She could see his soul in his eyes and she knew then that this man loved her. He released his grip on her hands and brought his to her face. She noticed that they were shaking and she felt a rush of pride. She could cause this powerful and sexy man to shake with need. She spun in his arms until she could wrap her arms around his neck and he immediately shifted back into one person causing her to chuckle. "Are you jealous of yourself?"

"Not at all," he growled. "But that was just the appetizer. You are about to be thoroughly fucked and I don't want my focus split." He lifted her off her feet before she could protest and headed in the direction of her bedroom. She did not bother questioning how he knew where her bedroom was. He had most likely been inside her apartment several times, without her knowing. It was funny how she knew now that he was holding her in his arms that he would never leave her unprotected. She had allowed her hurt and anger to cloud her reasoning, but in her heart, she knew Adio.

As soon as Annie's bed came into view, Adio tossed her on top of it with enough force that she bounced once. He held back a laugh as her blonde hair covered her face and she tried to fight her way out of it. She looked so adorably aggravated that he waited until she opened her mouth, most likely to berate him, to strip off his shirt. He watched as her look of irritation turned to hunger and a sense of pride welled in his chest. He wanted to tease her by slowly undressing for her, but he was impatient to be inside of her, so he quickly removed the remainder of his clothing. Annie pounced as soon as he climbed on the bed, catching him off guard. He fell backwards, and she landed on top of him. The mischievous look in her eyes was his only warning that things were not going to follow his plan, and that he was no longer in charge of this game. When she crawled down his body until her mouth hovered above his dick, he no longer cared who was in charge, and when her tongue snaked out brushing the head of his cock like a lollipop, he no longer cared about a single thing. Linking his fingers behind his head, he stared down, watching the show. She had straddled his legs, and was sucking his cock with her sexy ass stuck in the air making the entire scene appear like something from one of his most erotic dreams. Annie opened her jaw wide and he lifted his hips to meet her mouth as she sucked him deeper into her throat. Pleasure rolled down his spine and a moan fell from his lips as she hollowed out her cheeks, almost causing him to lose it right then. He needed this night to last. He needed her to remember, so once again, he shifted into two, having Mirage appear behind her. Mirage took Annie's hips between his hands, causing her to jump slightly in surprise, but she never broke her rhythm even as Mirage's dick slid inside her cooch. Adio and Mirage were one person in mind, and Adio could feel her tight wet pussy squeezing Mirage's dick, even as her hot little tongue stroked him to near insanity. She brought him almost all the way to completion before she tugged her mouth away. Their eyes met and held while a silent question passed between them. The lust shone brightly in her eyes, and he knew that she would agree, even before she allowed Mirage's cock to slip from her body. She crawled up the bed until she was straddling his hips with his dick buried inside of her all the way to the hilt. "Lean forward and brace your hands on my chest," he said, encouraging her into the correct position. She did as he asked and Mirage moved in behind her once more. Reaching between their bodies, Mirage ran his fingers through her juices, and wet his chosen path. He knew that she would accept him because he could feel how turned on she was. She wanted Adio in her pussy while Mirage fucked her in her ass and she was not the type to back down. Mirage went slowly, making sure that he did not hurt her, but once he was fully inside of her it was as if the entire room exploded in heat. The caresses came from several hands and mouths, until no one knew anything any longer. The fullness of her canals was so tight that it did not take long before cries of pleasure resounded from the walls. Annie collapsed into his arms, as he became one with himself once more.

As soon as Adio was back to being one man again, Annie snuggled up into his side. He held her tightly just as he had each night they had been together, and her heart squeezed in her chest at the memory. No one else could give her what he did, and she would never be able to love anyone else the way she did him. He was the one for her, but it did not change the fact that she was still trapped in the night.

"Why are you looking at me like that?" he asked, sounding concerned. "Did I hurt you?"

"Oh no," she rushed to reassure him. "It was amazing. It is only that I am trapped in the darkness now, and you're not. I can't ask you to stay in the night with me and if I go in the light then I'll die."

Adio shrugged. "I don't see the problem here."

"Well, you have to admit that this is no regular problem for a couple to have to get past."

"The hell it isn't," Adio shot back. "It is exactly like a couple who work opposite shifts. You have to work the nightshift now so I will work the nightshift as well. See, problem solved."

Annie was shocked into silence for a moment. His reasoning made things seem so ridiculously simple. He would switch shifts and they could be together like a real couple. "Why? Why would you do this for me?" She needed to know this final thing before she could give in to him.

"If things were the other way around, you would do the same for me, because you love me and I love you. There is nothing that I would not do for you, or give up in order to be with you, so just once, let me make you happy simply because it makes me happy to do so, please?"

Annie felt the sting of tears burning at the back of her eyes. It was true, she would have done the same for him, and so she would let him love her, because it was meant to be.

About the Author

Charity Parkerson was born in Tennessee, where she still lives with her husband and two sons. She is the author of several books including fifteen Amazon bestsellers.

Her "Sinners series" was voted one of the top ten best books by an Indie author in 2011- *Paranormal Romance Reads*

Her book "The Danger with Sinners" was named "Best Book of 2012" by *Paranormal Reads Reviews* and was a finalist in the 2012 Australian Romance Reader's Awards for Favorite Paranormal Romance.

Her book Wicked Sinners is a finalist in the 2013 Readers' Favorite Awards.

She was named as one of the top three Indie authors of 2012- *EbookBuilders* She is a member of The Paranormal Romance Guild, is a Goodreads moderator, a member of Coffee Time Romance, and co-host of The Melissa Craig and Charity Parkerson show. She won author of the week in August of 2011, and is a five-time winner of The Mistress of the Darkpath. She received two nominations in the eFestival of Words book awards for Best Short Story and Best Erotica of 2013

Acknowledgements

There are so many authors I would like to thank for all the help and encouragement offered to me along the way. Charity Parkerson, Charles E. Butler, Patti Roberts, Dionne Lister, Oleg Medvedkov, and C.J. Ellisson, without your compassion, wisdom, support, and help I would be light years away from publishing any book.

I would also like to thank Gary Morgan, your knowledge of vampires and movies are superb.

Thank you Beth at Bz Hercules for putting up with all of my neurotic insecurities and doing an awesome job walking me through this process and editing the book.

Lastly, to Joseph Napier, thank you for tirelessly putting up with me and my endless requests to reread the material for the umpteenth time. You always did so willingly and gave great feedback. You are my rock!

Much love,

Scarlette D'Noire

Now that you have taken the time to read this book, please post a review on Amazon.